I0575549

Spellbound

The Unrepentant : Book One

By : Olyvia Wyld

Spellbound Copyright 2025 by Olyvia Wyld
Published by Into the Wyld Publishing

All rights reserved. Printed in the United States of America. No part of this book may be used or reproduced without written permission except in the case of brief quotations included in articles or reviews.

This book is a work of fiction. Names, characters, businesses, organizations, places, events, and incidents either are the product of the author's imagination or are used fictitiously. Any resemblance to actual persons, living or dead, events, or locales is entirely coincidental.

No generative artificial intelligence (AI) was used in the writing of this work. The author expressly prohibits any entity from using this publication to train AI technologies to generate text, including, without limitation, technologies capable of generating works in the same style or genre as this publication. The author reserves all rights to license uses of this work for generative AI training and development of machine learning language models.

Cover Design: Samantha Bishop
Editing: Sorena Campbell and Alysha Thornton
Interior Formatting: Katiee Comer and Olyvia Wyld

Paperback ISBN- 13 : 979-8-99-30694-0-1
E-Book ISBN- 13 : 979-8-99-30694-1-8
1st Edition: October 2025

Dedicated to
all the ladies who get a little too excited
while running away from the masked men at
haunted trails.
I see you, I feel you, and this book is for you.

Spellbound is a masked stalker dark romance novel with subject matter that some may find upsetting. Please read the trigger list and continue at your own informed discretion.

Trigger Warnings

Consensual Marijuana Use
Consensual Alcohol Consumption
Profanity
Sexual Harassment
Religious Trauma
Past Child Abuse
Emotional Abuse
PTSD
Stalking
Home Invasion
Hidden Video Cameras
Explicit Sexual Content
Bondage and Blindfolds
Impact Play
Knife Play
Breath Play
Dub Consent & Non-Consent
Criminal Activity
Torture
Violence
Blood & Gore
Murder

Spellbound Suggested Playlist

Lips of a Witch - Austin Giorgio

Season of the Witch - Lana Del Rey

Bloody Creature Poster Girl - In This Moment

You're So Creepy - Ghost Town

Follow You Home - Nickelback

Final Girl - PI3RCE

The Fastest Way to a Girl's Heart is Through Her Ribcage - Ice Nine Kills

Let the Devil In - Green Lung

Morally Grey - April Jai

Curiosity - Bryce Savage

Closer - Nine Inch Nails

I'd Rather Burn - Blackbriar

You Put A Spell On Me - Austin Giorgio

Trick or Treat (Remastered Explicit) - Ghost Town

Oral Hex (Spell on You) - Bludnymph

RUNRUNRUN - Dutch Melrose

Chills (Dark Version) - Mickey Valen & Joey Myron

Love Bites (So Do I) - Halestorm

Till Death - PI3RCE

Table of Contents

Damian

Why did I let Sam drag me to a fucking party, Halloween or not? I don't need this. I hate shit like this. I know he can see I'm on the edge of going back, and he's trying to help or something, but this was stupid. Crowds make me antsy. Every time someone bumps into me, I want to knock them on their ass. The music is pounding in my head, making my fingers twitch in rhythm. The body heat and the stench of sweat are suffocating in this orange-fairy-light-lit, cheap-plastic-decor hellhole. It is all too close, too loud, too much. I have to get out of here.

The room is packed with people, dancing and grinding against each other in costumes. With all the monsters and ghouls, it almost looks like the actual hell that I feel like I'm in. I scan the room and see a sliding glass door leading outside to a patio on the far right. Sticking close to the wall, I work my way across the room, resisting the urge to hit any of the drunk idiots who keep falling into me. The porch light looks like a beacon, and I focus on it until I have the door handle in my hand and can feel the night air greeting my face. I don't take the time to even fully open the door, squeezing through sideways as soon as I can fit.

While I'm sliding it shut behind me, the smell of the sweat is replaced by weed and an intoxicating aroma of honey, vanilla, and...is that orchids? Instinctually, I turn towards it. At the other end of the porch is a woman, looking out over the railing. The porch light is illuminating her from behind, casting a long shadow across the yard, topped by the signature shape of a witch's hat. I almost step forward without thinking about it, but I catch myself. That perfume is sinking into me, seeping through skin, muscle, and settling into my bones. It is the most intoxicating scent I have ever smelled.

I can't see the finer details of her face in the shadows, but I'm still breathless from her beauty. I can sense it around her. She's pale, the porch light making her skin practically glow in the night. Her silhouette is elegant, voluptuous curves creating a feminine hourglass even on a strong build. I'd assume she is around 5'7", definitely athletic from how shapely her long legs are, but not thin. Her thighs are strong and thick, disappearing under the skirt of her dress, which pops out in that way that hints at what must be a beautifully full ass under it. The curve continues over her hips to a cinched waist, only to gracefully go back out with the swells of her breasts. An extreme asymmetric bob cut has her hair short on the back of her neck, but brushing her shoulder as it progresses forward.

The front edge of her hair touches her chest as it moves in the breeze. She's blonde with chunky purple streaks throughout like some 2000s emo heartthrob.

The woman is dressed as a classic witch in an elaborate costume. Her emerald green hat is covered in black lace, pieces of which are hanging sporadically from the brim. The dress appears to be a sweetheart cut, made of black velvet, with full-length bell sleeves, and black lace trim along all the edges. A corset covers the torso, accentuating her curves, made with the same emerald green, black lace-covered fabric. Even her heels match the green in the dress. Clearly, she enjoys the holiday, or at least dressing up, and knows how to highlight her figure.

She's swaying subtly to the music, lost in her own world as she smokes a blunt. The red glow of the ember reflects on something on her lip. Perhaps a piercing? It also illuminates her fingers, which have long, sharpened nails. Her left arm is resting across her body, under her breasts, with her right elbow propped up on her wrist. Her right hand lies lazily to the side, letting the blunt burn. She moves, almost dancing, as she exhales.

I don't notice women often. I tried dating when I was younger, but it was never genuine. I couldn't connect, and they either didn't know the real me, or if they did, they wanted me for the wrong reasons, so I quit looking. There's plenty of porn out there for urges, but as for women in my day-to-day, I just never notice anymore. But something about this woman is different. How could just stepping into her presence have such an effect on me? It's like she's magnetic. For just one delirious moment, I believe she might actually be a witch, out and mingling in the real world on the night she can hide in plain sight, because no human woman should be able to do this to a man. I am actively fighting the urge to step closer, but I can't take my eyes off her.

I don't know if she was feeling the same pull I was, or if it was by mere chance, but when she turned to me fully and my eyes met her deep green gaze, I knew that witch was going to either be my salvation or my damnation.

Celeste

The music from inside the house is muffled, but the bass carries through the walls and breaks the silence of the night. The deep and heavy beats reverberate through my bones as the crisp air raises goosebumps on my skin. I could've worn tights to stay warmer, but I love this costume too much to ruin the aesthetics over some chilly weather. I can hear April in my head, chastising me for my choice and saying "I told you so" in that sweet, melodic voice of hers. But it always sounds a lot more annoying to me when she's right. Rolling my eyes at her, even though she's not here to see it, I cross my arms, huddling close to try to stay warmer.

I raise the blunt to my lips, breathing deep. I don't partake often, but Halloween is a night for mischief and fun, right? The wind blows my skirt and petticoat over my thighs as I exhale and let the breeze take the smoke with it. *Damnit, it is cold.* I can't go back in there shivering or I'll never hear the end of it, so I start to sway to the music, dancing a little and letting my thighs rub together to work up some body heat. At least the dress is made of velvet, keeping my arms and torso warm.

I don't know why I splurged when I bought this costume. I don't ever spend this much on a one-time-wear type thing, but April was right (yet again) that nobody said I couldn't wear it next year as well...or for the next five years and it did look incredible. We both fell in love with it. She joked that the dress would make me a walking love spell and be completely worth it if it made Mr. Right fall in love with me tonight.

I sigh. Sure, then it would definitely be worth it, but that seems unlikely at a party like this. Don't get me wrong, I love this time of year. I'm a year-round-ghoul type girl, but I go hard on spooky season stuff non-stop for the eight weeks leading up to Halloween night. However, I tend to stay in and binge horror movies on the actual day. I tried buying candy to hand out last year, but my house is a small place on the edge of a couple farms, and no one ever showed. I was still eating my own candy at New Year's. But even when I decided against trying that again, I had planned to stay in because big random parties aren't my thing, and all the other attractions are just extra crowded on Halloween. But this year, April and Savannah weren't having it. Granted, they had different goals for me: April wants me to meet Mr. Right and have a happily ever after, while Savannah wants me to meet Mr. Right-Now and get laid. But they both banded together to get me out and now here I am, outside a *very* loud and overwhelming party at a stranger's house... and *very* thankful I thought to bring some weed.

I lift the blunt back to my lips for another hit. I let my hand hang in the air as I exhale in exasperation. The girls mean well, but this isn't the way. It's been three years since I left Issac, and I know they think that means I should be well on the way with someone else by now, but I had to find myself first, who I was without his influence and control. Because how the hell could I even know who my "Mr. Right" is if I don't know who *I* am? Honestly, I'm not sure I *do* know myself yet or if I'm even ready, but I'm too scared to tell them that.

I don't know why it was the thought of my own existential fear that made me suddenly more aware of my surroundings, but that's when I noticed him. A tall, broad-shouldered man is standing by the door in the corner of the porch. The orange lights shine through the glass and illuminate him in an eerie glow. He must be over 6'2", with extremely wide shoulders and a stocky, solid build. For a costume party, he went very simple with only a mask, a black button down, tight black jeans, and heavy-duty boots. But the mask more than made up for the rest of the simplicity.

It's truly terrifying. A warped depiction of a jack-o'-lantern is staring back at me, making my heart beat faster. It looks so real. It even has the texture of a pumpkin all over the face, down to the segments and the pitting in the "skin". The eyes and mouth are gnarled and ragged but appear solid black and hollow. There must be netting though, because I can see the steam from his breath billow out through the mouth. A black shroud hangs over it and covers the rest of his head, tucked into the neck of his button down. Even under his shirt and in the unusual lighting, I can tell that his arms are thick and muscled. His form seems tense like an animal ready to pounce. His hands are clearly balled up in his pockets, straining the fabric of the jeans.

How long has he been there, watching me? Who the fuck just does that? ...And why am I getting a whole different set of goosebumps from the thought of a sexy, mysterious, masked stranger watching me from afar? *Goddamn it, Celeste, get yourself together. Being into creepy shit doesn't mean you need to be a degenerate.* But then again, Halloween is a night for mischief and fun...

Before I even consider what I'm doing, knowing full well I will blame the weed in the morning, I turn to face him completely. "Are you going to stand there staring or come talk to me?"

Damian

The sound of her voice sends a chill down my spine. It's soft and alluring, but has a confidence behind it. A whisper from her would still sound like a command. The grace in her cadence almost daring you to defy it.

I can see her face clearly now that she has turned into the light and I wish to my core I couldn't. Her beauty is devastating. She has a sweet, round face that looks as innocent as a cherub's, but is gazing at me with a smirk that drips mayhem and sin. Between her beautiful green eyes, blonde hair, and that girl-next-door face, she could've shot someone in the street and still gotten away with murder if she claimed not guilty and batted her eyelashes enough. If she had kept a more typical aesthetic, that is.

I'm assuming she felt that her outside appearance hadn't matched her spirit, which is why she pierced her bottom lip in snakebites, one labret on each side, and added the purple streaks to an already bold hairstyle. I need to know who she really is. What makes a woman, who was born with looks that could've opened any door in the world, feel so out of place in that skin that she had to make it her own in spite of society's opinions or judgements. I need to know that woman, her story, her journey, and her soul.

The jewels in her piercings glisten in the porch light as her pouty lips move with her words. "If you just want to stare, I'm fine with that. But for your information, when I finish smoking this," she swirls her wrist, waving the blunt around in the air, "I will be going back inside into that big, crazy party and you may never see me again."

Fat fucking chance of that. I already know to my core that I will follow this woman to the ends of the earth if I have to. I don't know why, honestly I don't care. But I can't imagine going through the rest of my life dreaming of this stunning creature and never laying eyes on her again. It would put me in a damn mental hospital.

The urge to run to her side almost wins out, but I take calm, controlled steps over to her. I have to keep it cool, I don't want her to know I'm crazy already. "Well, talking to a witch isn't an opportunity I can allow myself to miss." I jolt at the deep reverberation of my own voice when I speak. I forgot the mask I purchased had a voice changer in it.

She leans back against the railing and holds out the blunt, offering it to me. I shake my head and reach into my back pocket to retrieve my pack of cigarettes instead, but I ask, "Do you have a light?" She eyes me curiously as she pulls a small set of matches from the neckline of her dress, her hand trailing along the swells of her breasts. My mouth literally waters at the sight. *What the fuck is wrong with me?*

"Are you going to smoke with that fucking thing on?" She looks at me incredulously as she opens the small matchbook from somewhere called Juke's Box. I didn't know places even had personalized matchbooks anymore.

I reach up and remove the velcroed-in black netting from the mouth of the mask and smirk, sliding it into my back pocket with the pack. I place the cigarette to my mouth and lean down, waiting patiently. I watch her eyes slide over the mask as I get closer with a look of intrigue, fear, and...a touch of arousal. *Interesting.* Is it the weed and the influence of Halloween fun, or is this something that actually excites my little witch?

Her eyes seem to literally glow with exhilaration as they move over the finer, creepier details of the mask and come to rest on my lips. She bites her own absentmindedly as she looks at mine, and my knees almost buckle with a need to kiss her. She lifts the matches suddenly and strikes one, cupping it to guard it from the breeze as I inhale to light the cigarette. But I almost drop it in the haze that takes over my head as her perfume hits me again with force. Inhaling deeply while so close to her was a mistake. There's no doubt about it, she's a real witch, whether she knows it or not, and I am under her spell.

"I'm Celeste," she offers casually, as if she hadn't just told me the name I'll be savoring the sound of on my tongue every day for the rest of my life.

I take a long drag and exhale the smoke as I speak. The voice changer is still working despite the mouth guard being removed, but my regular voice carries as well, making them mix into a new sound. "Hmm, seems very fitting."

She laughs, and my heart skips a beat at the sound. "Oh really? How so?"

"Celeste is from celestial, right? Meaning heavenly." I stare at her, and even though I know she can't see my eyes trained on hers, she is staring back into the black orbs of the mask so intensely I know she must feel my gaze. "And I have never seen anything that has made me want to thank God so much in my life."

Mentioning the big man in the sky immediately makes my skin crawl and brings to mind my mother's harsh squealing voice, screeching about sin and damnation. But I don't shiver or see red like I normally do with such memories, not while gazing into those emerald eyes. *Maybe Mother was actually right about something. She always said names have meaning, that they set a course for someone's life. Maybe Celeste was meant to be my heaven. Maybe that's why this attraction is so powerful. Maybe that's why we both ended up here tonight. Maybe...it was fate.*

Her laugh pierces the night again; loud, unapologetic, and infectious. "Who would've thought a witch could make a man more religious?" she says in feigned shock and conspiracy. She smirks that devilish grin again as she stubs out the end of her blunt on the railing, looking away as she does.

I don't know what came over me in that moment, or if her breaking our gaze had simply freed me from being paralyzed by her, but I drop my cigarette on the porch between us, stepping on it to put it out as I fill the tiny space that had been left before. One arm snakes around her waist, crushing her body to mine, while the other goes straight to her chin, grabbing it and forcing her to look up at me. "Do I look like a man to you in this?" A growl escapes from my chest as I feel that old monster inside me welling up. I want this woman more than I have ever wanted anything, and it is bringing out every part of me, good and bad.

I watch as her pupils blow wide like saucers and her breath catches in her throat. The shock on her face melts into passion. I'm surprised we aren't steaming in the night air due to the sudden rush of heat between us. My strong arm nestles perfectly in the crook of her waist, keeping her right where I want her. Those luscious curves fill out around my hold and pillow against my body. Just touching her while staring at that gorgeous face makes me rock hard. *Fuck, this woman is perfect.*

Her hands, which had fallen against my chest when I pulled her to me, tighten suddenly. The nails dig through my shirt and into my flesh enough that she might draw blood, and I love it. If she's going to bring out every savage part of me like this, then she needs to be able to give it back. But while I'm contemplating if she could scar me with those claws, she does something that stops me in my tracks, my mind flashing white and my knees going weak.

Her hands slide up my chest, tantalizingly, until she reaches the top button of my shirt. Her eyes burn into the voids of my mask as she undoes one and then a second, a scandalous smirk painting her lips. Her nails dance along my flesh as she moves her hands under the now exposed edge of the mask. I'm so lost in the sensation of her touch, such an addictive combination of velvety skin and sharp claws, that I barely catch her wrists to stop her from exposing more than my mouth as she peels it up.

Her hands drop, breaking my hold, and she snatches up fistfuls of my shirt in her grip. She kisses me, jerking my face the last few inches to hers. Desperately, crushing her mouth to mine as if I was air and she was breaking the surface from a long swim. But once our lips meet, her movements slow and calm. She breathes deep like she's savoring this moment as much as I am. Our kiss is slow and passionate. My hand slides gingerly from her chin to the back of her head, my fingers locking into her hair; tenderly, softly, but clear that I'm not about to let her go. My tongue slides out and runs along her soft, full bottom lip.

Fuck, she tastes like caramel. Which has never been my favorite, but now I can't figure out for the life of me why I never appreciated how amazing it is. This is the most delicious flavor on earth. *Celeste is my heaven. She must be.*

Pulling back for just a moment, she looks up at me and flashes that sinful smile before she leans forward to catch my bottom lip in her teeth. My heart skips a beat as she bites into my tender flesh and rakes them over the meat of my lip. I have to drop my hands and grab onto the railing to remain upright, gripping so hard to hold myself up I'm surprised I don't splinter the wood. *How can a woman have such an effect on a man...especially a man like me?* The things I've done and she can almost bring me to my knees with a kiss. It is insane.

As my lip pops free of her teeth, her giggle fills the air, and she dances back from me, light on her feet. She practically skips across the porch, her skirt swinging back and forth over her thighs, teasing the possibility of a peek at her beautiful ass. She stops when her hand lands on the handle of the sliding door. Glancing over her shoulder at me where I'm still leaning against the railing breathing deeply, chest heaving, from our kiss, she winks as she slips through the door and disappears into the party.

I stare after her. She probably thinks what she just did was a fun, wild memory she can dream about for the rest of her life. Instead, she changed the entire trajectory of it with that kiss. *Celeste will be mine by next Halloween one way or another. Whether the process is a daydream or a nightmare is up to her.*

Celeste

Almost Ten Months Later

Driving home is typically the most boring and least favorite part of my day. It's nothing but me alone with my own thoughts for half an hour and that is never a fun combination. However, today, as I get to the edge of town, I see a bright orange banner announcing the location of where the pop-up Halloween store would be this year and my spirit lifts immediately. All the major stores have been pushing the spooky merchandise out for weeks, but this is the sign that the season is *really here* even if it is still hot as hell outside.

It is the middle of August and Halloween is about ten weeks away now. In my opinion, this is the absolute best time of year. You can taste the magic and the frivolity in the air. Life as an adult sucks most of the time, but something about the leaves changing and fall seasonal activities always brings back the joys of childhood. How can you not laugh when you are elbow deep in pumpkin guts or wandering in circles in a corn maze? It is just in time too, God knows I could use some joy in my life right now.

Don't get me wrong, I'm in a good place overall and very thankful for that. I have my health and security, but I feel like I'm missing that *spark* that we all crave. I work two jobs that I enjoy, one as a chemistry lab assistant at the local community college three days a week, and then I bartend Saturday through Wednesday nights down at Juke's Box. It's a redneck, hole-in-the-wall type joint, but the regulars are reliable and decent people. Joe may get wasted every Tuesday night and retell the stories of his high school football days yet again, but he never tries to grab anyone's ass and always tips me fifty percent, so why the hell would I complain? I also have my own house, which as a single, twenty-nine year old is impressive in this economy.

When I made the decision to buy this old farmhouse out in the sticks, I knew I was going to have to fix it up. I was actually really excited about that. If it needed renovations anyway, then there was no reason for me to feel guilty about spending money to turn it into my dream home. But what I *didn't* consider is how long of a drive it was every time you are in the middle of a project and you come across some small thing you need and don't have. After my fifth one-hour round trip while trying to redo the porch, I was second-guessing myself.

I spend most of my free time doing home improvement projects. At this point, the people I bought it from probably wouldn't recognize it. With help from my friends, Savannah, April, and Eric, April's fiancé, I have taken the old run down shack and made it into a gothic little cottage nestled into a series of cornfields instead of a forest. There is still some detail work I want to do, but the bones of the house are now what I always envisioned growing up.

It's a small, one story, two bedroom, one bath home. The first thing I did when I moved in was paint the whole thing black with white trim on the shutters and rebuild the porch. It now wraps around three sides of the house and is fully covered. Classic cottage-core wood detailing runs along the edge of the roof and the railings, but takes on a slightly darker feel in the black. I let the ivy grow wild up one corner of the porch, near where the swing is. I love the touch of whimsy it brings.

Inside reflects the same energy. My floors are linoleum that look like grey stone tiles and the black walls continue throughout the house. Houseplants are in every room, practically taking over, in silver painted vases of all shapes and sizes. My living room has a lush white, grey, and silver rug on the floor, surrounded by giant bean bag chairs and cushions in a variety of deep jewel tones, silver, and black. The one time my family has visited me since I bought the place two years ago, my father complained that I needed to get "real furniture", but with only Osiris and I in the house and the rather small group of friends I have over, I really don't see the point.

To some, my living room might be better described as a social library. The long wall opposite all the windows to the front porch and eclectic seating is made entirely of bookcases. The interior of each cubby is painted white to better highlight the treasures inside. I do have quite the book collection, but about half of the spaces are filled with oddities. Most people think it is creepy, but I love collecting animal skulls, preserved insects, organs in jars, and art made from such remains. The other walls are covered in horror movie posters and inspired art and Osiris's elaborately arranged platforms and scratching posts.

Osiris is my very spoiled, very entitled orange tabby with green eyes that match my own. I don't know if that is what really sealed the deal for me when I met him at the animal rescue, but I do know when I looked into those eyes I felt like I saw a bit of myself in them. He came home with me that day and has made himself king of the castle ever since. He isn't very fond of visitors though. It took the girls coming over regularly for practically a year for him to stop running away every time they entered the house.

He usually retreats down the hall from the living room to either my bedroom or my "home theatre". I am being very generous with that term. Since I only needed one traditional bedroom, I turned the other one into a movie lover's haven. I have the walls covered in the rest of my movie posters and shelves upon shelves of my DVDs. Movies from every genre and time period of filmmaking are included, but my horror collection gets the spotlight, sitting front and center on the shelves surrounding the giant 85" TV mounted on the wall. That was a housewarming present from my parents. I have a long, low dresser I upcycled into an entertainment center under it with all the electronics and two large leather double recliners in the center of the room. A small snack table sits between them. I also paid for a surround-sound speaker system to be put in as my Christmas gift to myself the year I moved in.

My bedroom may be small, but the aesthetics never fail to warm my soul. The walls are covered in black and white photography and art in sleek silver frames. My bed is a four poster canopy made of silver rails with grey, silver, and black brocade fabric and matching pillows over my black satin sheets. I don't bother with a duvet or blanket; my body tends to run hot, so I'd just kick it off anyway. Matching nightstands bookend the bed, and a large full-length mirror hangs on my closet door. The dresser at the end of my bed holds my collection of toys and spicy books, but I don't get much time to use them. Some of the stuff in there hasn't been touched since I left Issac almost four years ago now. I've been alone ever since, so I have no idea why I bothered to put all that energy into completely covering my ceiling with these mirrored tiles. Hopefully one day they will finally see some use. It would be hot as hell to watch myself get railed properly for once.

My bathroom and kitchen are still rather untouched other than the floor and paint. Renovations don't just take time, they take money, so I have to pace myself. Since these are the places I personally spend the least amount of time, they were the bottom of my priority list. My small, stacked washer-dryer combo is set up in one corner of my bathroom, taking up what little space there would've been outside the bath/shower, toilet, and standing sink. I have a small table for up to four people in my kitchen that I use on the rare occasions I cook. Most of my food is straight from the fridge or a can and microwave ready if I'm honest. When I'm trying to be healthier I'll pick up some deli food in town on my way home, but if I had to cook fresh for myself everyday, I'd probably starve first. April brings over food sometimes because she "feels bad" I don't eat as I should.

My best friend means well, but she can be a little overbearing at times. We met in college at UNC Charlotte about an hour from here. She is actually why I settled down in Ammerton, North Carolina. This is her hometown. After I graduated with a Chemistry degree, I just couldn't bring myself to go back to California and sink into some random lab job for a pharmaceutical company. My parents weren't exactly thrilled at first but they have come around in the years since. April, Eric, and Issac were all in-state students so it was an easy choice to stay near the people I'd grown close to while I figured myself out. I moved in with Issac first, but when I left him, I came to Ammerton to live with April. I stayed with her for two years while I saved up to get my own place. She and Eric were so sweet about it, but everyone could tell they were excited when I bought my house so they could move in together. He proposed six months later and they are getting married this December.

April's over at my house a lot, though. When Eric moved in, he told her that he would handle all the bills so she could focus on her photography career. She's very talented, but living in a smaller town does tend to limit the clientele. Only so many people are going to get married each year or have the guts to do a boudoir shoot. Unfortunately, this leaves her with plenty of extra time to fuss over me.

As I pull into my driveway, I notice what has become a familiar sight on my porch. A shiny black box, with a large orange bow sitting on top, rests on my stoop. Instinctually, I look around, but the corn fields have grown up to six feet on either side of my property and I can't see anyone. Not that I ever have before. I sit in my car just staring at the present, my heartbeat quickening. I'd forgotten it was the first quarter moon again already.

It took me a few months of receiving these gifts to piece together when they were arriving. At first it seemed random, it was a different day of the month, a different day of the week, etc. But then I noticed they kept showing up around the same time in relation to my period, but since that made no sense I started considering other cycles on a similar timeline. By the time the fifth gift came, I was certain it was tied to the moon cycle. Whoever was leaving me these gifts was always coming on the first quarter moon.

I received the first one near the end of last November. A cute plastic cauldron filled with all my favorite candies. Since the box was clearly hand delivered, I'd assumed it was April or Savannah trying to help me out of the post Halloween blues, but they both vehemently denied it. At first the girls were excited at the prospect of my having a secret admirer, but when I pointed out this was delivered to my house, which is in the middle of nowhere, and that I've not brought or told any man, other than Eric, where I live, they were suddenly more concerned for me.

At first I was worried Issac had found me and was trying to be "sweet" as a way back in. But after almost a month went by and I was left another gift anonymously I knew it wasn't him. Issac might be able to fake being sweet and caring to get what he wanted, but he was never one to be patient or not take credit for something. That gift had been a box full of various gemstones, raw and polished. There was a gorgeous geode of amethyst in there that I had tried to resist the urge to put up on my bookshelf, but I failed. If I did have some weird stalker, putting up this stunning rock or not was not about to change how the rest of this played out. I'd seen enough true crime shows to know that much.

I decided to wait to call the police until the third one arrived. I know that cases like this are hard enough to get taken seriously at any point so I felt I needed a pattern before I even tried. However the cops treated me like I was the girl crying wolf when I called them out and there was a ceramic bat watering can inside. I tried to explain that I wasn't concerned about the *contents* of my gifts, but that I was getting random packages *delivered to my house* by someone unknown. They told me there wasn't really anything they could do. If I physically saw someone suspicious on my property I could call 911 and they would respond, but otherwise there was nothing else to be done.

In the months since, I have received a variety of gifts: plants, sage, a tarot deck, books, etc. All thoughtful gifts that fit me, I must confess. On a few more drunken nights, I'm embarrassed to admit I've entertained the thought of meeting my admirer and letting him have at me. I know it is fucking crazy and the man may well be a psycho who is going to kill me one day, but he has spent almost a year asking for nothing while simultaneously putting more thought and care into gifts for me than any partner I've ever had. Part of me wonders if this man could actually be in love with me, but then the smart, reasonable side takes over to remind me stalkers are unwell and most likely incapable of love. Statistically, he doesn't even know me and has fabricated an entire fantasy of me in his head and is obsessed with that, which if I were ever to shatter would cause him to devolve and murder me.

I sigh as I exit my car. I really have watched too much true crime. A few months ago, I was getting really bad. I could've sworn I had left a cup in the sink that was cleaned and put up when I got home, and I freaked out calling April and Eric convinced the guy had been in my house. I was locked in my car with a kitchen knife when they got here and Eric cleared the place. No one was there and there were no signs of forced entry. There also weren't any signs of forced entry the next two times I called them out over my DVDs being in the wrong order and a plant being in a different spot than usual. I knew I was getting too paranoid when even April told me I was being kinda jumpy. So I stopped paying attention to the little things I thought I noticed. But the gifts...no one could convince me I was being crazy about those.

Standing over these boxes always feels like a combination of victory and dread. Victorious in the fact that I am not crazy, that there *is* someone out there with some kind of unhealthy obsession with me. But the dread would always creep in as well, because I never know when opening one of these might end up killing me, and yet my curiosity won't allow me to just leave them alone. If one of these blows up some day, just put "The Cat" on my headstone.

I sit down on my top porch step and bring the gift to my lap. It is surprisingly light for such a large box. Maybe it's ricin and I'm about to die very painfully right before the start of my favorite time of year. Honestly, that'd be my luck. Survive almost a whole year with a stalker just to get murdered right before all the fun starts. I take a deep breath in and hold it, like that would actually do anything, as I untie the bow and carefully lift the lid to look into the box. But in the next moment I am squealing and tossing the top aside to get into it quicker.

My present is one of the most beautiful necklaces I have ever seen. It's a velvet choker with a delicate silver chain draped in swells along the center of the band. There is a very large stone charm hanging from the middle on the same type of chain. One half appears to be onyx and the other opal, creating the look of the first quarter moon within it. The weight of the stones confirm that they are real and once I have it on, the charm sits right above the line of my cleavage and the choker rests along the bottom of my neck. It wasn't until I looked down at the charm resting on my chest that I noticed, for the first time in over eight months, there was a note inside the box.

"TRICK OR TREAT, MY SWEET. SEE YOU SOON."

Damian

The corn stalks are itchy as hell, but I don't care. It's easy to hide among them and they allow me to get closer while I watch Celeste. Seeing her put the necklace on excitedly today made me so ecstatic I almost ran out of the field and snatched her up. She was giving me a claim over her. She's a smart woman. She may not know who I am, but she knows these gifts are from a stalker and yet she not only accepts them but she gets excited over them...at least when she thinks no one is watching.

I've seen her complain about them to her friends, and I won't lie, the time she called the cops hurt my feelings a little, but I reminded myself that she doesn't know me yet, doesn't know what we are meant to be. She isn't rejecting our future, she's just being smart. I'm sure this scares her a little, but then again, I've learned that my Sweet loves being scared.

I started stalking her right after Halloween last year. The way Celeste invaded my mind, body, and soul in that one night is nothing short of black magic. There is no other explanation. I don't think she even did it on purpose, but she has this power over me and no one holds dominion over a demon without using some dark shit.

I went to Juke's Box the very next night, prepared to go every single day until she happened to wander back in, just to be pleasantly surprised to see her behind the bar, sporting a right arm full of tattoos that her dress had hidden the night before. All black and grey artwork of various scenes from movies broken up by realistic roses. At the time, I couldn't identify the movies, but there was a mattress with a fountain of blood exploding from it, a view from between a pair of legs framing a fresh grave and shovel, a silhouette of a hulking figure with a machete along a treeline, etc. Even without knowing the references, the art was compelling and high quality. She clearly invested in her work.

We are the same in that way. My entire torso, front and back, is covered in blasphemous religious iconography. It was one of the first things I did when I left home at sixteen and got involved with Kage. It was my way of dealing with all the fucking religious bullshit I'd had beaten into me as a child once I was out in the world finally accepting the "demon" my mother had always said I was. But I did have the sense to invest in the best artist I could find. Quality ink therapy is expensive, but it's also permanent and worth the investment.

I remember being irritated as hell that she was even hotter than I had realized. Part of me had stupidly hoped it was just the magic of the evening and when I finally saw her again that she wouldn't be the enrapturing creature I met in the dark the night before. I wanted that spell to be broken. I *needed* it to be broken. I knew damn well that while I have olympic levels of self-control, if I faltered for even a moment, then I was going to do something stupid like actually kidnap this woman. But instead she was even more stunning as her typical self and I knew there was no hope for me...or her.

I learned quickly that she's a very pleasant bartender, who's good at her job and thus in a place like that, is very familiar and friendly with her regular patrons. It didn't take long to overhear all sorts of pertinent details about her life. Everyone there calls her Cee Cee, which I personally enjoy. I'm assuming it is short for Celeste Carroll, however Celeste should be reserved just for me. She is my heaven after all. The men that fawn over her in that bar should be grateful I even let them look at her. It would be in their best interest if they don't push their luck by speaking her true name.

I spent the next couple of weeks figuring out her schedule and following her around town. When I finally managed to tail her out to her house without looking too suspicious, I was shocked at how remote and alone she was. Immediately, I was worried about her safety and if she would be able to properly defend herself out here because the cops would take forever to respond. It took me longer than I wish to admit to realize I was doing exactly the kind of shit I was worried might happen. Except I know I would never hurt her, not in any way she wouldn't enjoy at least.

I became consumed with worry for her. If she had captivated a terror like myself so easily, then what other monsters in the night might she attract? For all I knew, she was a magnet for unhinged, violent men. I couldn't leave her alone. I was spending every evening outside her house for practically the first two months. It was messing with my work, but luckily owning my own electrical service company gives me some leeway. As long as I'm making sure men are showing up to the jobsites and contracts are being completed, it isn't a big deal if I'm not the one literally doing the labor. But I knew sleeping outside her house was risky and unsustainable long term, so when she left to spend Christmas in California, I seized the opportunity.

When I first learned about this trip, I was tempted to book a flight and follow her out there. The idea of not seeing her for five days made me sick to my stomach. I didn't know if I would mentally survive it. I hadn't gone a single day since we met without seeing her. But the likelihood of being inconspicuous out there was slim and I needed to do some stuff here while the house was empty anyway so I stayed behind.

I watched her leave for the airport midafternoon. She slipped the spare key she was leaving for April under one of the plants on the front porch before she left. I waited until I was certain she was gone, grabbed the key, and took it to a local hardware store in town to make a copy at one of their machines. It's wild to me that you can just copy any key, anonymously, at a random machine. It makes crimes like breaking and entering far too easy. I had taken, copied, and returned her spare key in under ninety minutes. April didn't even come to get it so she could take care of Osiris and the plants until the next morning. I've had the freedom to come and go from Celeste's house as I please ever since, and it is a privilege I partake of as often as I can.

The first day Celeste was gone, I watched to see when April would be coming by in the mornings and evenings, so I knew when I could safely be in the house setting up surveillance. Before she got back from California I had a camera in every room of the house. Hiding the small, inconspicuous ones in vents and the elaborate shelves built into the walls was easy. She hasn't noticed them yet, and they have been there for almost eight months now.

I set up the feeds to stream to my phone and from there I can cast them to any TV in my place as I wish. I've been able to sleep in my apartment now that I can watch over her from my own bed. But I'm still out in these fields a lot. I can't help myself. I have to be near her. I *crave* it. I've filled my apartment with orchids and bowls of honey so that it smells more like her, but it's not the same as wandering through her house where her intoxicating aroma permeates the air.

I always get rock hard from that perfume, reliving that kiss in my head over and over. I've been patient and made due with touching myself while watching her for so long, but I won't deny the fact that it gets harder to resist her everyday. I can't wait to have my hands on those supple curves while I taste my Sweet again...to savor every part of her soft flesh. The image of her laid across those silk sheets, body arched and head tossed back as she grinds on my face, screaming her release on my tongue, has me adjusting myself in my jeans as I work my way through the corn to return to my motorcycle. I rip off the possessed pumpkin mask I had been sporting the night we met as I go. I always wear it when I'm out here, just in case she happens to see me.

I've been working my way into her life in a more typical manner as well and I can't risk her recognizing me, when she knows my name and face. Damian LaCroix, the older student in her Chemistry 111 lab class. I enrolled at the local community college last January as a part time student pursuing a two year transfer degree so that I could take the Chemistry course she works as a lab assistant for. As much as I enjoyed watching her at home and occasionally wandering into the bar, I needed to see and understand all sides of her. Enrolling in a college course was nothing if it allowed me to be close to her and watch her in a whole new light.

It was worth every penny. Not only because I got to savor a twitch in my cock every time I had to call her Ms. Carroll, but because she is absolutely brilliant and showcases her saintly patience with these idiot children that struggle to follow basic instructions. I was ready to slam their dumbass heads into tables ten minutes into every lab, and they weren't even asking me their questions, but she'd just flash that devastating smile and answer every inquiry with grace. She is going to make an amazing mother to our children one day. The summer has been long, but the new semester starts next week and I've already ensured I'm in her lab again for the Chemistry 112 course.

I pull a small caramel from my pocket and toss it in my mouth, a habit I started to fend off the urges to taste her again before the time was right. I check on her via the cameras before I get on the bike where I won't be able to see her for another twenty minutes. I live on the very edge of town, but I still don't like just how far in the sticks she lives...even if it does make my hobby easier to get away with.

She's curled up with Osiris in the theatre with a blanket and a bowl of chips, watching some slasher flick I can't make out on the screen. I have spent a lot of time in that room over the last few months. I was never allowed to watch any horror movies growing up, just like I never participated in Halloween as a child. My crazy zealot of a mother thought they were the devil's handiwork, and as I was already a tainted soul in her eyes, she would have no additional stains on me in hopes that a merciful God might still allow me into Heaven. The thought is comical now, especially knowing that even though I may not have watched blood and guts get spilled on screen, I have spilled them myself in real life. Even after I got involved with my cousin Kage, collecting his debts and handling problems, I never did get around to watching horror movies. They just didn't matter. But after my first walk through of Celeste's house, it was clear they were a passion of hers, which immediately made them extremely important.

Just one stroll through her place and anyone can tell my Sweet is a spooky, creepy girl. I have to admit I wasn't expecting all the dead things as home decor the first time I walked in, but then again, I should've guessed; she is a witch after all. Her horror movie collection is massive and she had made quite the impressive home theatre, so I figured it would be a waste not to watch them at her place a few nights a week while she was working at Juke's. I find them enjoyable, maybe even a little cathartic. I walked away from Kage a few years ago, and Sam gave me a new lease on life, but that rage and bloodlust still lives in me. I have had to resist it periodically ever since I quit, but more so since I met Celeste. Anytime someone disrespects her, even brushing by in the grocery store without saying excuse me, it makes me want to break their kneecaps so they have to kneel properly to apologize to her. So watching these gory slashers work their way through a mass of typically stupid, irritating people is a relaxing outlet. When I realized that, I thought I had figured out why she liked them so much.

However, it didn't take me long to figure out that she may not have repressed bloodlust as much as she has repressed kink. I will never forget the first time I tuned into the cameras to find her in her home theatre, riding a dildo to one of the films. I almost came in my pants the moment I realized what I was witnessing.

She was in nothing but a large t-shirt, completely naked underneath, which I had learned was typical for her when she is home alone. One hand slid the shirt up so she could massage her breast, showing off that stunning form as she was perched on the edge of the double recliner. The fabric fell to perfectly frame the shape of her body, draping alluringly along her waist and continuing back over her hips, bunched up on top of her delicious ass. I immediately made this feed fullscreen on my TV. There was no way I wasn't going to enjoy the hottest porno of my life on a proper screen.

The dildo was suctioned to the leather and she was moving her body with an erotic grace I swear I had never seen before. I couldn't help but imagine her hips gliding back and forth on me like that as I furiously jerked off while watching her. My cock was out and in my hand without a thought. Something about this woman reduces me to pure instinct and need. Later I would rewatch this video...and the many more to come so I could learn her body and how she likes it to be played with, but no matter "why" I watched them, every single time would end with me cumming, crying out her name.

It was driving me crazy that I couldn't hear her moans and gasps through the camera as she was building her orgasm, but her face showed it all. Eyes locked on whatever bloody chase scene had her worked up into a tizzy, her beautiful mouth falling open in those little cries that I would've sold my soul to have heard in that moment. Her legs were trembling from her growing arousal as she braced herself by holding on to the front edge of the recliner with her other hand, her nails straining the leather. Her breasts were bouncing in sync to her hips. She is a fucking goddess. Even without hearing, smelling, or touching her, I came harder than I ever had before when I watched her back arch and she bit her lip as she shook in release - all the while her eyes never leaving that screen.

That's when I started planning for this season. If my little Sweet loves to be scared, then why wouldn't I sweep her off her feet exactly how she craves? I know she's a good girl. She wants to be normal and accepted by society, so she tries to hide those darker instincts while pretending she's owning herself entirely with the hair, clothes, piercings, and tattoos. But *I* get to see the parts she tries to deny until she can't hold back anymore. If she cums that hard from watching another woman run from a man in a mask, I can just imagine how she will spasm and squeal on my cock when her very own masked nightmare claims her in every way a dark, depraved witch deserves. She is exquisite and I intend to help her accept all the darkest parts of herself because if she can learn to love her own darkness, then she can love mine. And whether she knows it yet or not, I have no doubt that she yearns to do just that.

Chapter 4

Celeste

"You know I love you right, Cee? So I say this from a place of genuine concern," I sigh as I wait for Savannah to drop whatever great insight she has for me today. Her tone falls from the sing-song sweet cadence of her "concern" to a deadpan as she continues, "You should be really worried about any dude you bring home who can maintain a hard-on while surrounded by all this dead shit." She visibly shivers in her inverted position hanging off one of my giant beanbag chairs, her fiery red hair spilling all over my floor. "It is fucking creepy. I'm afraid you're going to end up screwing a psycho."

I roll my eyes at her. I twist back around to the antique chandelier I thrifted, that is currently sitting in the center of my living room. I've been trying to figure out how the hell I'm going to put it up all day. "Yeah? Well maybe I want a psycho. Normal men are gonna take my mask kink as a personal insult or some shit," I tease back, hoping to stop this conversation before it gets any real traction.

She jolts, pushing herself upright in mock offense, her hand flying to her chest. "What? It's just the truth Cee. I deal with weird ass men all the time. You have no idea what is out there."

Savannah is another bartender at Juke's, that's how we met, but she also moonlights as a cam girl online. Not that I blame her, she's a petite, redhead with a stunning face, pretty light green eyes, freckles, and perky little curves the men lose it over. She makes more in a month online than we make in three from tips working at the bar.

The hilarious part is she is *solidly* gay - like, kissed a boy once in high school and very decidedly knew guys weren't her thing gay. She says she resorted to her imagination and music videos for release until after she moved out of her parents place and could come out. There isn't much of a lesbian scene in Ammerton, but she often rides out to the city about an hour away to meet women when the mood strikes, though personally I've never seen her be serious about anyone.

I do know that she's had to deal with some real fucking crazies online though. At Juke's, an asshole might get handsy, but we don't get death or rape threats over doing a job they are actively paying for. But I can't say I believe that her critique is entirely from a place of experience and not from her personal distaste for my oddities.

April's high pitched voice carries down the hall from my kitchen, "Really? You think she doesn't know about what kind of crazy is out there with that 'admirer'," she spews venom as she draws the word out, "of hers?"

Savannah and I exchange a glance, this time for her to roll her eyes at me. Savannah thinks April is blowing the gifts out of proportion and that it's not that serious, meanwhile the newest development of the note saying "see you soon" has April convinced she should go ahead and plan my funeral since I refused to call the cops. I tried explaining I didn't see a point when they would just tell me there was nothing they could do again...and decidedly left out the part where I didn't want to call the police because the note had sent a chill right down my spine and straight to my clit.

April bounds back into my living room carrying three glasses of her infamous sangria and I greedily snatch mine up, well aware that I'm probably going to need this with where the conversation seems to be headed.

"I still can't believe you are staying out here after that last present. You know you and Osiris are welcome to come stay with Eric and me, right?" She looks at me in earnest and for a moment my heart swells. I love her, I do, but even if I wasn't somewhat intrigued by the idea of finally meeting this stalker, there's no way we'd all survive trying to coexist in that tiny apartment.

"I am not about to let some random dude run me out of my own house. Hell, I'm almost done with making it my perfect little gothic cottage, I'm not going to just ditch it now because some freak has a crush." I toss myself into one of the other chairs while April stares down at me, her chestnut curls framing the frustration on her face. She's literally tapping her foot at me. *Ugh.*

Savannah's keen eyes are trained on me and I focus on the fruity white wine mix in my glass to keep from looking at her. April ends up sitting crosslegged on the floor in front of me and suddenly I'm very aware that I've got myself backed into a corner between the two of them. I notice Osiris sitting up in his tower across the room and I try to psp psp psp him over to me for back up, but the jerk just lifts his head lazily to give me a look that says "you got yourself into this mess, you deal with it" before laying back down.

Both of the girls are staring at me, waiting. Scrambling, I toss my glass back and down my entire drink. I go to stand up, saying, "Oh, hold on I need a refi-"

"Oh no, here, take mine, I insist," Savannah says dramatically as she takes my glass and shoves hers into my hand.

I cut my eyes sideways at her as I mumble out a thanks and try to retreat deeper into my chair before I let my gaze glide back over to April who is staring at me like a detective in some old noir film. I'm surprised she doesn't have a lamp shining in my face at this point.

"Cee, seriously. What are you going to do? This is dangerous."

I groan, "I don't know, okay? I don't have a set plan. But as much as no one here wants to admit it, if this guy wanted to kill me, I'm sure he has had plenty of opportunities to at this point."

"Or she."

"What?"

Savannah smirks. "You said 'He has', I'm just pointing out that it may be a woman, you don't know."

I blink in response. Honestly, I hadn't even considered that. I mean, the idea doesn't make me any less wet, but it definitely is a change from the image I've had in my head during my more drunken escapades.

"I don't care if it is a man, woman, or a motherfucking alien, you've got to take this more seriously, Cee. Look, I know I've gotten a little complacent about it with you over the last few months, but this is an escalation."

"Fine! But what do you suggest I do? Besides abandon my own house because that is *not* going to happen." I'm already halfway through this glass of sangria and really regretting sharing this newest development with the girls.

April seems to consider my question for a moment before she answers me. "I know the cops have dismissed you before, but do you have any new ideas about who this might be or why they might be doing this? Any patterns or info?"

"Well, the gifts always come on the first quarter moon."

Both the girls look at me a little shocked while I explain how I finally pieced that together, but Savannah threw me when she asked, "do you know where you were the first quarter moon before the first gift arrived? That kinda sounds like an anniversary type gesture."

It took me a moment to process that. I feel so stupid. *How the hell had I never bothered to check into that before?* Next thing I know, I am struggling to reach the phone in my back pocket when April interjects into my train of thought to declare she was already on it. I try to sit back and relax. Instead, I end up clinging to my glass, gently swirling the wine and watching the fruit dance inside as I wait for her to conclude her internet search.

My eyes leap up to her when I clock her movement in my peripheral vision. She's holding the phone screen up to Savannah whose face drops in shock and wheels to stare at me.

"What is it?!" I practically scream, immediately embarrassed for the loss of composure but too frantic to really care.

"Cee..." April starts.

"The first quarter moon before your gift was Halloween!" Savannah finishes with as much barely contained energy as I am feeling at the moment.

I sit back in my beanbag as I'm flooded with the memories of that twisted pumpkin mask, a kiss that tasted of rum and smoke, and walking away from a man I have dreamed of over and over again ever since. The same man that I had gushed to the girls about on and off since last year? The same man I had confessed I absolutely regretted not giving my number to? The one we had joked about going back to the same party to look for this year because his memory might just haunt me the rest of my life? I mean, sure, there were nights I imagined they were one in the same while I touched myself, but that was just a fantasy...a really fucked up, twisted fantasy... *They can't really be the same man, can they?*

I don't know what came over me, but I was on my feet and walking towards my front door mumbling something about 'no it can't be' before I even realized what I was doing. April was quick, right on my heels and grabbing my arm to stop me. She wraps me up in a hug, telling me how it will all be okay and maybe she could reach out to other people she knew at the party and someone might know who he is. That we might be able to catch him.

In that moment, I was so happy April and I were embraced and she couldn't see the way my face fell at the thought of my pumpkin prince possibly being arrested instead of kissing me again...but as my eyes meet Savannah's over April's shoulder, it is very clear that she noticed my fleeting despair at the idea. Damn, that bitch notices everything.

Damian

The buzz of the tattoo machine is the only sound in the shop as Darren works on my right forearm. He agreed to come in early to meet with me. I try to schedule anything I have to do during the morning hours when I can't be with my Sweet anyway. But even now, I'm watching her and her friends in what looks to be an intervention. I smirk.

Did she slip up and tell them that she might actually be enjoying my attention? Do her silly little friends think they can talk sense into her? Keep her from me? I can feel my smile growing more sinister at the thought. These girls have no idea what they are trying to meddle with. No one stands in the way of fate. I've long given up on the idea of a real God, but I do believe something made Celeste just for me and, friends or not, no one will keep us apart. I know they matter to her, so I am trying to be patient, but these girls better not push their luck. I will remove any obstacles I need to before I risk losing her.

I am prepared to spend every second left in my life convincing Celeste of the truth if needed because of her own doubts, but I will not tolerate pests in her ears keeping her from fully accepting me and herself. Because deep down my precious Sweet is just as twisted up as I am. That's why she loves this time of year so much. This is when she can flaunt that side a little more, like kissing a mysterious stranger in a mask like he was air, without judgement or side eye. Her soul is laced with that mischief and darkness, she just needs to be with someone who can make it safe for her to accept it all the time. My poor Sweet has had to wait far too long for that, but I'm going to make it well worth it.

I tear my eyes from the screen long enough to check on Darren's progress. He's almost done, currently adding in the white highlights, and as always, his work is on point. Celeste's visage now graces my arm. Her beautiful form perched atop a pumpkin, leaned back on one arm and legs kicked out in front of her, the other hand holding the witch hat in place behind her head in a classic pin up vibe. Her curves embody the art style perfectly. The simple black dress he drew her in is small and fitted but covering everything in the right places.

I'm going to have to wear long sleeves in class and at the bar over the next couple weeks, but at night when I'm chasing her, making her heart race and her thighs slick from the fear and excitement, I want her to know how much I treasure her. Even if it feels like I might kill her in our dangerous little games, she will be able to see that she's gotten under my skin. That she is as much a part of me and my story as everything else that marks me.

The feed on my phone disappears as a call begins to ring through. Sam's name lights up on the screen and I accept, sliding the phone up to my ear. "Hey, what's up?"

His gruff voice crackles across the line. "Nothing much, just thought I'd reach out and check up on you. Ryan and the boys say that they haven't seen you in a few days."

I sigh. I'm going to strangle those guys. Sam is too old for them to be worrying him like this. He's in his sixties now. Still strong and healthy for his age, but stress isn't good for anyone at that point. I can practically see him running his rough calloused hands through his mop of white hair repeatedly, concerned that I've "fallen off the wagon". The way he uses that phrase around the guys, I'm sure they assume I'm a former addict of some sort...which I guess I kinda am, but I doubt they assume my vice was violence.

"I'm fine, Sam. Just busy getting ready for the upcoming semester. I'm actually with Darren right now, squeezing in an appointment before life gets crazy again."

I hear the slight exhale of relief and the relaxation in his voice when he replies, "Oh shit, I didn't know you were getting something new done. Good for you, kid. What is it?"

My jaw clenches. *Shit.* "Just a pin up girl, something classic and sexy." But I knew when I said it he wouldn't buy that. He knows me too well.

The beat of silence on the other side of the line is deafening as we both face the fact I'm lying and that he can tell. "Hmm well, if Darren is doing it, it must be killer. I'm excited to see it, kid. Be sure you swing by my place in the next couple days to show me, don't make me come hunt you down."

Before I can get my agreement out, the chime on the front door goes off. Both Darren and I look up immediately to see two big burly motherfuckers bust in. The second holds the door open for a tall, lean man to stroll through the threshold. Fitted three-piece suit, snappy wingtip shoes, and a flashy stud in one ear, his hair is cut close to his head now and his face has hollowed out some, but those cold ice blue vulture eyes haven't changed.

"Hey, cuz, long time no see." His warm, broad smile would look disarming to the general public, but I know him better. That's the look he gets when he's reeling someone into a gamble that he is certain they are going to lose. He's only that fucking toothy when he smells blood in the water.

Sam's voice is still in my ear. "Did I just hear Kage? Damian! What the hell are you -" his voice cuts out as I hang up and place the phone down on my lap calmly. I hold Kage's gaze and Darren reads the energy in the room, quickly wiping down my arm and wrapping it up. He excuses himself to the back and Kage takes the opportunity to come sit down in the chair next to me, that same slick smirk on his face that always meant there was something he wanted from me.

"Kage." I greet him coolly.

His laugh cuts the air, sharp and short. "Oh? That's what I get after all these years? Come on, man. I heard through the grapevine you were going to be back in here, so I thought I'd swing by and see you." His eyes drop to my new favorite piece. Quirking an eyebrow in interest he adds, "Though it seems like your taste in art has changed..."

The hairs on the back of my neck are prickling. I stand up, grab my shirt, and start pulling it on as I reply, "A lot has changed, Kage. It's been almost ten years. What do you want?"

He sits back in the chair, legs spread and arms crossed, as he watches me in amusement. "Just wanted to catch up. See how life is treating you. Curious if you are still feeling this whole 'working man' thing?"

My fingers are twitching with the desire to knock him right out of that fucking stool. His two guards are standing back at the door. It doesn't appear they came armed, probably Kage's idea as a way to keep me more 'relaxed'. *Idiot.* I could have him on the floor and that tattoo machine shoved through his eye socket before they got over here. Then I'd deal with them.

But that would be messy and draw more attention than I need. The tattoo shop may not care whose money they are taking for their work, but I have a feeling they aren't going to be down for helping me dispose of some bodies. I can't balance trying to evade murder charges and making Celeste addicted to me, and she will always be the priority. So, as much as I hate it, I reign that instinct back. I can taste my own blood as I bite my cheek hard to regain control.

I don't even bother to button up my shirt. I pull a few hundreds from my wallet and toss them on the tray, not caring to look back at him. My voice is cold and steely, "You know what hasn't changed Kage? I don't like fucking surprises. So next time you want to have a ten year reunion, fucking call first."

I step around him and walk straight out of the shop. Even though I don't glance back, I can sense him watching me. I pull a caramel from my pocket and pop it in my mouth, hoping the taste of Celeste will calm my nerves. *Fuck, I really don't need this shit right now.* I'm so close to actual happiness and suddenly my past is going to try to stroll right back into my life? *No.* But as much as I dread it, I have a bad feeling that it isn't going to be long before I see him again.

Celeste

I didn't notice I was chewing on the end of my pencil until a small feminine voice carried over all the lab stations' hood fans, breaking my attention from the safety forms I was filing.

"Ms. Carroll? I'm sorry, but I don't see the right size beaker at our station."

My stool scratches across the floor as I get up to help find a beaker that I'm sure will magically be there as soon as I am the one to look for it. I pull my lab goggles down over my eyes from where they were resting on my forehead as I start to move through the room. It's only the third week of the semester and I'm already frustrated with half of the students in this lab section. I can re-explain a concept that someone doesn't understand till I'm blue in the face with no issue, but incompetence drives me crazy.

I take a deep breath and remind myself that most of them are still children. Suddenly being able to vote and sign themselves into debt doesn't actually make someone mature and grown up. I put on my sweetest smile as I reach her and her lab partner. They both look like babies. Hell, I'm not sure he could even grow stubble on his chin yet, which makes it much easier to be kind when I bend down to look in their cabinets and discover the right beaker sitting front and center.

I hand it to them, content with the embarrassed blush that they seem to be sharing. Though as I turn to head back to my paperwork, she speaks up again, timidly but with hope in her tone "Hey, are you planning on going to the fall kick off festival this weekend? I'm part of the art club and we're doing this really cool live sculpture thing and I think you'd enjoy it."

I smile. This happens every year. Lab assistants are typically younger, more relatable, approachable, and understanding than the professors, so we always end up with a few students who want to make friends. Some of my peers hate it, but personally I think it is adorable, so I always try to be as kind as I can with them.

"Oh that sounds awesome, I really wish I could go, but I already have plans this Saturday."

"More home improvement projects, Ms. Carroll?"

My pulse quickens and I jump slightly at the smokey sound of Damian LaCroix's voice behind me. Instinctually, I turn to him. He's settled at the station behind these kids. He was in one of my labs last semester as well. Now Damian is certainly not like my typical students. I would assume he is in his thirties, probably looking for a career change. He's registered as a transfer path student. Definitely the quiet type, but the few times he has spoken to me, he always mesmerized me with this taunting smirk like he knows something I don't. He's way too handsome to be gifted a smile like that as well. It's not fair to the other men on this planet, honestly. He has a chiseled jaw he keeps clean shaven and thick black hair he styles like fucking James Dean. But the shot to the heart is his eyes. He has thick natural lashes that would make any woman envious, framing these molten hazel irises with subtle streaks of red in them. The first time he asked me a question in class, I'm embarrassed to admit he had to repeat it because I completely lost my train of thought looking into them.

While he looks like a fifties movie star in the face, he's built like a freight train of a man. Large and broad shouldered, he looks hulking hunched over the stone slab that makes up the station, perched comically on a stool far too small for his form. His arms fill out his long-sleeved shirt in a way that makes me certain he could pick up just about anyone like a sack of potatoes with no problem. Leaning forward on his crossed arms flexes his chest in a delectable way. I wonder what his pec would look like with my teeth marks in it?

Fuck, Celeste! Focus. I stammer trying to remember exactly what we had all been discussing. "Um...no, no. A date with a pumpkin patch, but I do have a feud currently going on with this chandelier that I can't figure out how to hang up in my living room. If I don't get it done before Sunday, then I'm probably going to just resell it and move on."

I swear that there's a shift in the atmosphere, almost like the air itself is suddenly heavier. It feels harder to breathe under his gaze. But when I run my eyes over him, the only changes I can see are that his hands look like they are balled tighter and his eyes seem...I don't know how, but they seem darker. Despite that, the same knowing grin paints his face as he offers, "Why don't I come over and help? I'm an electrician."

I'm pulled from my analysis of his body language, surprised at this new little nugget of information. "Oh, that's cool. Uh, I mean, I appreciate the offer, but I don't really have the budget for a professional right now."

"No worries. I'm happy to do it for free. You've helped me more than enough in these classes to earn it. Let me pay you back. It's the least I can do."

I should've said no. I should've told him thanks but you are a student and that could be seen as a conflict of interest. I should've told myself don't invite a student, grown man or not, that you want to lick the sweat off of, back to your house no matter *what* he's offering. But instead, I thanked him profusely, gave him my address, and made an appointment for him to come over tomorrow afternoon.

Damian

My fingers are battering against my steering wheel as I make the drive out to her place. I've had music blaring constantly since yesterday, but nothing is drowning out all the screaming in my head. "A date with a pumpkin patch" or was it a "a date, with a pumpkin patch". *Have I been too distracted lately? Did I miss some asshole worming his way into her life while I've been setting everything into motion?*

The fields are zipping by outside the windows and I glance down at the speedometer. *Damn.* I relax on the gas pedal because otherwise I'm going to be getting to her place in ten minutes flat and I need more time than that to compose myself.

Play it cool. It won't be helpful to upset her. I need answers, so that I can handle whatever...*obstacle*...has decided to worm its pathetic, unworthy way into my Sweet's attention, but she doesn't need to know I did it. At least not until after she's fully stepped into the darkness with me. Once Celeste has gotten over her fear of the 'dark', we can stay up all night in it sharing every secret and sin we wish, but I don't want to scare her...*too much* before we get to that point.

It was never part of my plan to be spending time with her as my public self. But I just reacted with that offer to help her in a stupid moment after the damn date thing. *I should've just hung this fucking chandelier while she was at work and made it her next gift.* Now instead, I've increased her interactions with me on two different fronts and put myself at a higher chance of being found out before I'm ready. Practically a year's worth of fucking planning and I put it at risk in a moment of weakness and jealousy? *Goddamn amateur hour. I'm fucking rusty.*

The rest of my drive to her place is spent making a mental checklist of all the things I need to do to not slip up and reveal who I am. Don't go anywhere in the house without asking where it is first. Act slightly surprised by the decor, in the very least, in body language. Don't be too familiar with Osiris...can't control what that little asshole does, but that shouldn't be enough to make her too suspicious.

Just keep it casual, like you would on any other job, and make small talk about Saturday. It'll work out. I carefully pull into her driveway and immediately kick myself for not passing by first and having to turn around, it would be more believable. However she's not outside and the charade wouldn't have been seen anyway. *Fuck. Breathe, before you make shit worse.*

As I climb out of my truck, I close the door loudly, making my presence known and taking my time collecting my tools from the back to give her a chance to come and greet me outside.

"Hi, Damian!" Her beautiful voice carries excitedly from the porch as soon as I hear the front door open. When I look over, she is bounding across the planks, a smile absolutely lighting up her face. Even from across the yard, her eyes are shining with warmth and excitement. Despite all this time, my heart skips at the sight. *She really is stunning.* Watching her actually look back at me from that porch, happy and welcoming, brings a natural smile to my face.

She's sporting a tight Camp Crystal Lake Counselor t-shirt over a long sleeve fishnet shirt and a pair of jeans that look painted onto those curves. She's already put on that sexy black lipstick she always wears when she's headed to Juke's or going out with her friends. She looks just like the cool, rockstar, final girl she wants to be so badly...the one I plan to make her feel like. The image of her on her knees, holding me captive with those eyes as she smears that lipstick up and down my cock, invades my mind. I almost groan out loud. *Fuck. Get it together.*

"Hi, Ms. Carroll," I try to sound friendly, but the sudden straining of my pants has me slightly grumbling in discomfort. I pull a caramel out of my pocket and pop it in my mouth to help fight off the urge to kiss her.

She doesn't seem to notice. "Oh no, please call me CeeCee outside of class. You are helping me out here, no need for the formalities."

I don't want to call her what the masses call her. She is my Celeste...my heaven. I'm not about to soil that with a nickname that dampens the weight of her tie to me. "Well thank you, but I think I'm just going to stick with Ms. Carroll," I meet her eyes as I walk up to her, my tool bag swung back over my shoulder. "If you don't mind, that is. I would hate to get too comfortable and call you something else in class by accident. We wouldn't want to start any rumors." I wink.

She laughs. That infectious, beautiful sound filling the air around us. "Good point. Better get inside quickly before someone drives by and sees you," she gestures out to the wide expanse of fields and the empty road while raising her eyebrows conspiratorially. *Is she just funny or is she trying to protect me from her stalker? Either way. Adorable.*

"Lead on."

She swivels on her heels, guiding me inside. I purse my lips in a way that I hope is giving *"Interesting. This is a choice."* once we step into the living room. I actually love it. It is her, inside and out, and I live to watch her express herself in any form. All I want is for her to be happy and to be mine. Everything else in life at this point is flavor for her enjoyment.

She tucks a piece of hair behind her ear timidly, "Yeah I know it's a lot. Most people don't get the appeal, but I guess for me, finding beauty in death gives us each meaning beyond our brief blips on this planet. If we can still bring joy and beauty to the world even after we're gone, then maybe our mistakes in life just don't mean as much."

I stare at her. All this time watching her, following her, and trying to learn everything about her and she still surprises me. "That's beautiful."

Our eyes meet for a brief, intense moment. She seems to be searching for something in mine, before her cheeks flush and she stammers out, "Yeah, uh - yeah anyway, the chandelier is over there," gesturing to the very obvious ornament sitting in the middle of the floor. "Let me know if there's anything I can do to help. Would you like something to drink? I have lemonade, Cheerwine, and water."

"Lemonade sounds great." I don't really want a drink, but it feels like she could use the moment to herself. "Then really all I should need is someone to protect me from that ferocious beast over there," I toss my head in Osiris's direction. He's coiled up on top of his tower peering at us inquisitively. Little dude isn't used to seeing us both at the same time, I guess.

She smirks as she struts out of the room. "Osiris, be nice to our guest while I'm getting him a drink. I better not have to clean up another one of your messes. Getting the blood out of the rug took *forever* last time."

I can't help but smile at her cheek. That sass is going to get her into so much delicious trouble eventually. But I set about the task at hand while she's busy so that I can focus more on our small talk when she returns. It's a simple rewiring job for anyone who knows what they are doing. Probably about an hour's worth of work max, should still be more than enough time to figure out what I need.

At least it would've been if her phone hadn't rang right when she was coming back with my drink and she was on a call for over forty-five minutes with April. *It really is a good thing she is so fond of that girl.* Celeste seemed very uncomfortable and to be giving clipped vague replies, so I assume April was talking about the stalker and she didn't want to give away too much in front of me. *Funny.*

I'm almost done and debating with myself about how I can drag this project out more when she finally returns. "I'm so sorry about that. I had to take that call, though."

"No worries," I smile warmly at her, "I can't blame anyone for wanting to talk to you."

She flushes again, that cute pink rushing to add color to her cheeks and neck. "Oh, thank you...So, umm, how is it coming?"

"I'm almost done and I haven't been mauled by the cat yet, so I'd say pretty well."

Her eyes flit over to Osiris, who is now snoozing away inside his tower, before returning to me. I can see the wheels turning in her head and I'd kill to be able to read her mind, but I settle for the small smile that finds its way to her lips.

"Very brave of you to face such a threat to help me out. You'll have to let me treat you to a real drink sometime as a thank you."

A devilish grin, dripping sin, spreads across my face. I can't help it. "Why, Ms. Carroll, I thought you already had a date to a pumpkin patch this weekend and now you are asking me out? How *scandalous*." I mock-whisper the last part, reveling in the way her flush deepens into a dark red.

"No! Damian, no, I wasn't asking you out. I also work as a bartender at Juke's, and I just meant you could swing by and have a drink on me." She's flustered, tripping over her words and I love it. It's so satisfying to bring nervous little reactions out of her.

"Ohhh," I drag the word out in a condescending way, "well, if that's all you meant, then I guess I'll settle for a free drink as a consolation prize."

She rolls her eyes at me as I finish with the last screw and climb down the ladder. I fold it up and move out of the way so she can admire her newest home addition. The way her emerald eyes glow with wonder makes me want to put one up in every room of her house.

"What do you think?"

"I love it...wow. It is perfect. Thank you so much!"

"Anytime." I say it naturally, because I mean it, but she catches on to the weight behind it. She sneaks a glance at me before she looks away when she catches me staring at her. The urge to snatch her up and kiss her passionately is creeping back into my mind. I feel like an addict who can't outrun their temptations as I pop another caramel into my mouth.

"You must really like those."

I almost choke, but quickly compose myself. "I mean they are okay, more of a habit. Had to do something when I quit smoking." I shrug. That *isn't* why I had started with the candies, but I was going through them so constantly at the beginning, that I ended up quitting just to have a cover for the caramels with the men at work.

"Oh, well congrats. That's a hard habit to kick."

My voice drops just slightly as our eyes meet again, "You have no idea." The energy between us is electric and I know we can both feel it.

She starts to shift her weight back and forth between her feet uncomfortably. "Well...yeah, definitely come by Juke's and I'll treat you. I work Saturdays through Wednesdays. But I'm sorry I have to finish getting ready for work tonight so I -"

"I get it, no worries," I assure her quickly, packing up my stuff as she nervously picks at her nails.

Her eyes keep shifting up to the chandelier though and even in her nervousness she can't help but smile and my heart swells. That's all I want to do - put that smile on her face every day, whether that means doing home improvement projects or chasing her in a mask.

And that's what I'm going to do, no matter how much convincing it takes. I know she will love everything I do to her in the end. I get so lost in all the ways that I could put that smile on her face that it takes me until I'm five minutes back down the road to realize I didn't learn a single damn thing about Saturday.

Fuck.

Celeste

The glow of the dashboard clock is mocking me with how much later it is than I planned. Getting home after three in the morning on my days off is not typical for me, but April landed this big boudoir photography contract with someone in the city and she wanted to celebrate. So I did what a good friend does and tossed on a sexy little black dress to hit the town with her and act like a couple hellions. I wasn't about to rain on her parade by dipping early, thus here I am, up late despite having both day plans *and* work tomorrow night. Ugh, my bed is calling out to me like a siren's song. I stopped drinking around midnight so I would be good to drive, but the alcohol has still made me sleepy and those silk sheets sound like heaven right now.

Actually, I'm so tired that not only do I pull into my driveway, but I am halfway out of my car before I register the loud screaming coming from inside my house. Instinctually, I slam the car door closed and lock it. Snatching the kitchen knife I've been storing in my console for months now, I start to dial 911 on my cell. But before I hit the call button, the screaming is drowned out by a very familiar creepy, gravelly slasher's voice. I stall. What the fuck?

Leaving the numbers cued up, I lay the phone on my lap so I can crack my car window and listen carefully. The mocking dialogue and cackles continue over the screams and pleas. *Goddamn it, that's fucking* Nightmare on Elm Street. Knowing that some poor girl isn't getting gutted in my house at the moment allows me to lean back in my seat and take a deep breath. But the instant my eyes close in relief, I jerk up again. *What the fuck is wrong with me?* Just because some random girl isn't getting murdered doesn't mean *I* won't be. Clearly, my stalker has decided to break into my place and not even be subtle about it...which honestly makes me more nervous.

I glance back down at my phone. I could hit call and report this. Throw my car into reverse and take my ass back into town to wait at the police station while they investigate. That's the smart move. *That's what you* should *do, Celeste...* So why is it that my leg is bouncing rapidly with nervous energy and I've got a death grip on this knife like I am about to go see exactly who is in my house all on my own? I don't even have to answer myself. There's no way I'm going to resist a chance to see who has been stalking me, especially now that it might be my pumpkin prince from last Halloween. The question is, if it *is* him, what am I going to do?

I know what I *should* do. I should stab him. I should turn him in to the police. I should make myself safe again and move on with my life. But the way the thought of him waiting for me on the other side of that door not only deliciously quickens my heartbeat, but leaves my panties dripping wet, means I am probably *not* going to do what I should.

Carefully, I exit the car as quietly as possible. Searching the corn desperately, I ease the door closed behind me. Not that I'd have a fucking chance in hell of seeing him if he was waiting to ambush me out here. It's almost the new moon and that sliver of light in the sky barely makes the house visible in the night, it's certainly not enough to pierce the shadows of the thick stalks. I'm just going to have to throw some elbows and kicks if he grabs me from behind and pray that gives me the distance I need to turn the knife on him.

I work my way across my yard to the porch slowly, trying to listen for any tiny sound, but the deafening blasts of the movie makes it impossible. My skin is prickled in goosebumps and I steel myself against the slight tremble making its way through my body. As I take the doorknob in my hand, I look back over my shoulder once more, scanning the edges of the fields. I test the handle to find it unlocked. *Goddamn it. He's toying with me.* My heart feels like it is going to burst out of my chest. I wouldn't say my blood is running cold, more like thick. It almost feels like it has weight within my veins. So why am I so hot and flushed? What the fuck is wrong with me? *If I make it out of this I seriously need to start therapy.*

Breathing deep and holding it in, I fully turn the knob and ease the door open. The house is completely dark, except for a flashing glow illuminating the hallway outside the theatre, whose door is ajar. The movie is even louder here, reverberating off the walls. *Could he really be in there?* He's been smart enough not to be caught for ten months, why would he just be there waiting for me? Except he *did* say he'd see me soon... Could he be ballsy enough to just break into my house and make himself at home while he waits to introduce himself? *How crazy* is *this motherfucker?*

I step in fully, closing the door. The click of the latch makes me physically flinch, but considering the blaring movie, he shouldn't have heard it. I check Osiris's tower as I pass to find him curled up inside, hiding from the noise. At least, this psycho isn't dumb enough to fuck with my cat, then I would stab his ass, living twisted wet dream or not.

I slide myself down the hallway silently, barely lifting my feet and stepping back down like I'm trying not to crush feathers understep. The closer I get the more disorienting the volume is, I can barely hear myself think. At the threshold, I place my back against the wall steadying my breathing so I won't get winded as quickly if this gets physical. *Come on Celeste, you can do this.*

Breath. *One.* Another Breath. *Two.* Again. *Three...*

I whip around, swinging myself through the doorframe, to come face to face with an empty theatre. The screen is illuminating the room and myself in a cool blue hue. It is also back lighting a piece of paper taped to it. All my well intentioned breathing prep escapes me as I start to hyperventilate. Scrawled in heavy, thick lettering is a message that says -

"I WANT TO PLAY A GAME, MY SWEET.

HIDE AND SEEK.

CAN YOU FIND ME BEFORE I COME FOR YOU?"

Holy shit. What the fuck am I doing? I run across the room and snatch the note up. Almost as if there would be a chance that it could dissipate in a cloud of smoke and this will all turn out to be a liquor induced dream. But that didn't happen. The paper crumples in my grip as I tremble, mocking me for needing to confirm this is fucking real.

I hit mute on the remote so I can actually hear myself think. Maybe even have a chance at hearing him move through the house if I'm not too deaf at this point. I could barricade myself in here and still call the police. But it'll take them twenty minutes or more to get out here. Can I hold him off that long, especially if he knows I contacted the authorities? This man seems very...*determined*. I don't know if a door that doesn't lock with a couple recliners against it is going to stop him. No, that's not going to work. Maybe I -

Suddenly a loud clattering comes from the kitchen, startling me. *Fuck!* I whip back to the door, knife out in front of me in a panic at the sound. I bite my lip, clicking my teeth against my piercings. *Screw him.* If he wants to fucking play games, then let's play. But if I find him, then I'm going to stab him, see how much the sick fuck likes that.

"Fine. You wanna play, huh? Then ready or not motherfucker, here I come!" My yell carries across the house, bouncing off all the walls, but is met with silence.

I adjust my grip on the knife, refusing to let the thin layer of sweat that has broken out on my palms mess with my traction. He wants to scare me. That's what freaks like this get off on and I refuse to give him that.

I storm out of the room, quickly glancing left down the hallway to the living room and my bedroom, before turning to the right to pass the bathroom and go into the kitchen. I'm not bothering to sneak at this point. I want him to know I'm coming for him. If he plans to kill me tonight, then I'm going to take his ass with me.

As I reach the threshold of the hallway that dead-ends into the kitchen, I immediately scan the room. There's no obvious figure just standing in the open, but I do see a pot I had left out laying on its side on the floor with Osiris sitting up on the counter licking himself contentedly. *Goddamn it, Osiris!*

I spin around to check behind me in a panic as the image of being jumped from the back while that damn cat just sits there calmly fills my head. I then walk backwards into the kitchen, but no one is there. I glance over to see that no one is under the table as well. Even if he was small enough, he couldn't fit in the cabinets without tossing out a lot of shit in the process so it seems the kitchen is clear. For a moment I consider trading my knife out for a bigger one, but I decide against it. Bigger may seem more appealing while imagining stabbing him, but in reality a bigger weapon will be less wieldy in close quarters.

I lick my lips, trying to wet them though my mouth has gone dry as I step back into the hallway. I should just clear the house from one end to the other at this point. It is small, there's only so many places the bastard can hide.

When I reach the bathroom, I throw the door open with all my strength, hoping to shove it into him if he is hiding behind it. Instead it collides with the wall, the slam echoing through the house. The shower curtain is pushed back already and the tub is empty. I slip backwards through the door, returning to the hallway.

I turn my attention to the bedroom. I've already been through the living room and the theatre. It's not impossible that he moved without me noticing, but it seems unlikely. The closer I get to my room, the more the hairs on the back of my neck rise. It feels like rocks are forming deep in the pit of my stomach, but I know that there is something waiting for me in there. However, I pause at the door. Not because I'm scared to face him at this point, but because that feeling in my guts isn't just dread. *Fuck. Should I be more scared of him or myself at this point?*

The door creaks open as I enter the room. Every side of my canopy bed is closed, the fabric ties hanging loose from each post. I glance up to the ceiling mirrors trying to see into the center of the bed, but the angle cuts off halfway down the canopy. If he's laying low, then I wouldn't be able to see him from here. I take a single, deep, ragged breath before I decide to just go for it. I clear the distance to the bed in three steps and jerk the fabric back with the knife raised, ready to strike.

"TOO LATE"

The words on the note don't even have a chance to fully register before I feel his rough grip on my wrist holding the knife, twisting it around on itself so sharply my arm strains and my grip on the handle loosens in a blink of an eye. His other hand snatches me up by the back of the neck. My free hand flies to his instinctively trying to break his hold on me, a small gasp escaping me in the shock.

His hold is demanding, completely in control of my head. I can't even turn to sneak a look at him. He is squeezing the tender flesh of my neck from the back; not to the point of pain, but with enough force to make me certain he could snap it if he really wanted to. I can't tell if it's his grasp or the fear that is making my body seize up in resistance. Not that he seems bothered either way. His center is molded to my back, filling in every gap made by the bend of my spine and the curve of my ass. Every one of his muscles feels tight and tense like a predator poised to strike. His form is massive, making me feel small in comparison. The heat of his skin is scorching through my dress causing my mind fog over. *Fuck, is he shirtless?*

He aggressively shakes my right arm, making the knife slip from my spasming grip and clatter to the floor. As soon as the blade is out of my reach, every part of his body seems to relax against mine. Every part but the hand on my neck.

A deep, dark voice breaks the tense silence and for just one moment the sudden weakness in my knees makes me thankful he's holding me up. "Tsk tsk, my Sweet. You probably should've thought it through before you decided to make weapons fair game." His other hand slowly trails down from the wrist of my outstretched arm while he speaks, as if he's cherishing every single goosebump he has given me.

The touch has me trembling, but not from fear...*well, not* only *from fear.* Every inch of skin his fingers have dragged over is tingling. Electricity overriding my nerves and shooting straight to my nipples, making them strain against my bra. I feel him lean in closer, his breath hot on my flesh. His face is buried in my hair and the moment he breathes in deep, smelling me like someone savoring a fine wine before they taste it, I instinctually let out the smallest of moans.

I have a split second of silence to realize what I just fucking did and pray to God he didn't hear me before his deep rumbling chuckle in my ear makes it very apparent he definitely did. *Goddamn it, Celeste. What the fuck is wrong with you? Stomp on his foot, toss your head back into his, throw an elbow to the gut, do* something *logical before this screwed up fetish gets you killed!*

But as if he could read my mind, he expertly moves his body in unison with me as I shift to throw an elbow into him. Stepping back from me quickly, he lets go of my neck to shove my left shoulder, feeding into the momentum of my attack and sending me into a full spiral. My elbow clips him, but he doesn't slow. His hand is on my throat again in less than a second and he pushes me back into the bed, my knees buckling against the edge as we collapse onto it.

I forget how to breathe as I'm suddenly face to face with that same demented pumpkin mask that has been haunting my dreams. *It really is him, and now he is here to haunt my reality.*

"Don't worry, next time I'll be sure to bring my own to play with."

Damian

Her chest is heaving against me, her mouth hanging open in a pant but she's silent like she can't manage to actually catch her breath. That stunning face froze in shock and fear the moment she saw the mask. Her body though...I can read the arousal all over it. A pretty little flush has brought color to her chest and neck, the swells of her breasts now bright pink. Her hands are on my back, those threatening little claws digging into my flesh. I can even smell her sweet arousal as it permeates the room, mixing with her perfume. But most apparent of all is her eyes. The pupils are blown wide in excitement, just like that very first night and that makes my cock twitch in my jeans.

I push myself up on my right arm, lifting the top of me a few inches from her. My hips now bear my weight, resting on hers to hold my feisty woman in place for her lesson. My left hand stays on her warm throat, though I'd much rather put my lips there. *But I have a plan and I need to stick to it, no matter how badly every cell in my body wants to consume this woman like the forbidden delicacy she is.* I can feel her pulse beneath my grip and it threatens to make me feral.

I've done many fucked up things in my life, however I have never been aroused by the violence before. Yet the way her body responds to the force and the fear is awakening new tastes inside me. My mind races with all the things I could do to her right now to relish in her screams and her orgasms, but that's not the point of tonight. I bite the inside of my own cheek to regain focus as I stare into those emerald eyes, refusing to allow myself to be tempted more by examining her exquisite body.

"Look at the trouble you've gotten yourself into," I say as I slide my hand up her neck to her chin, leaning out of the way and holding her still so she is forced to watch her own reactions in the mirrors over the bed.

Her hands rush to the front of my chest, trying to shove me off balance, but there's no point. My Sweet is strong for her size, but I'm so much bigger. I don't want her to stop trying though; there's something tantalizing about the way she's fighting so desperately even against my stillness, while I make her watch the panic and desperation on her face. *I hope she leaves some claw marks as souvenirs.*

"You're so pretty when you're scared," the deep rumble of the voice changer echoes in her small bedroom. "Look at the way your eyes glisten as they well up. Is that why you get turned on by your scary movies so much? Do you think those women look just as pretty as you when they are scared?"

The shiver that runs through her body makes me hiss. "That seems like a yes, my Sweet." I lean in close to her ear, the mask brushing against her as it moves with my mouth. "I'd feel guiltier about those tears if we both didn't know that I am making that pussy weep just as much." Her eyes widen in shock and shame, making it very clear I'm right.

She gasps and I squeeze her chin, forcing her jaw to stay open and cut off the sound. "Listen carefully my Sweet, I'm only going to tell you this once. Your safe word is 'trick'. Now don't get me wrong, you are going to be mine eventually. I will make you *desperate* to give in to me...*and yourself*...but if any individual night goes too far, then say 'trick' and I will stop partaking of my treat." The mere thought makes my voice rumble in a growl.

Her heart is pounding so hard I swear I can hear it, but it's probably the way her pulse is racing under my grip that makes it so apparent. Her eyes strain to look to the side at me. I can feel her jaw trying to move, so I release my hold and trail my hand down her body. Savoring the path it makes moving over her voluptuous form as she shakes lightly beneath me.

Right as my hand reaches the hem of her dress and brushes her soft, velvety skin I hear it. A soft, unsure, "Trick."

Every muscle in my body is revolting, but I pull my hand back and move myself over her, staring. Letting her gaze into the black void of the mask's eyes as I resolve myself. The silence and the tension as she questions if I'm a man of my word is its own form of tease. Her eyes are a mixture of arousal and fear, just the way I love them, but she needs to know that she will always have the power over what happens to her body in the end. *Now her life is a different matter, but we will get to that later.*

I take one ragged breath before I lift myself off her and the bed. I depart silently, leaving her behind in a mess of body and mind to find her own way out of the new world I just threw her into.

Celeste

Normally all the families and kids running around the pumpkin patch brings a smile to my face, but after being up all night, the screeches and squeals are just adding to the headache.

Last night couldn't have been real.

But I know it was. I spent the rest of the night laying wide awake trying to process what the hell happened...and why I had the reactions I did.

I confronted my stalker and it turns out he actually *is* the sexy stranger I met on Halloween last year. We kissed once and this man has literally followed me, left me presents, and probably been in and out of my house for almost a year? *That's fucking crazy, no matter how good the kiss was.* Why couldn't he just dream about it a couple times a week like I did? That's what sane people do.

Then he breaks into my house and sets up a sadistic game of cat and mouse just to fuck with me? He scares the shit out of me, has me ready to stab him, and practically has my life flashing before my eyes, just to walk away with a single word from me?

What the fuck.

I really have no idea what to make of him or what he actually wants from me. Stewing on it for hours hasn't helped me either. Is this some long game, where he wants to toy with me before he kills me as another way to get his rocks off? Or does he actually think he can make me give in to him like he said? *Could he really be crazy enough to think this shit will make me fall for him like we are in some fucked up fairytale?*

Yet as much as I want to act incredulous towards such an assumption, I spent just as much time last night questioning myself as I did his motives. He wasn't wrong about how turned on I was. I was fucking soaking and trembling...and deep down, part of me didn't want it to stop.

That scared me more than he did, which is why I said "trick." I never would've used the safe word for what he was doing if the situation hadn't been so *absolutely batshit insane.* My treacherous, apparently death-wishing body was eating that shit up, but I know that's not fucking okay. So does he, yet he seemed so at ease while...I mean, there's no sugarcoating it, *assaulting* me. Labeling it that just made the guilt swell and I groan internally. *Ugh. I need therapy.*

A pair of children cut in front of me suddenly, almost colliding with me, as they prance between all the pumpkins. I jolt to a stop and their parents call out an apology, embarrassment plain on their faces but I wave them off. No need for more guilt to mess with the energy here, certainly not over kids being kids when there's already real fucking degenerates trying to come to terms with themselves bringing the bad vibes with them.

Every year I come to the same pumpkin patch as a date with myself to kick off my seasonal celebrations. It's a local farm, and the Jacksons have always been kind to me. They let me borrow a small pull wagon to carry all the pumpkins I inevitably pick out each trip, and they've given me pretty decent discounts for several years now. I like them.

A pumpkin on the next row catches my eye. It's nice and fat, but very squat as if something had been laid on top of it while it grew. Perfect for carving some long, horizontal scene - maybe a graveyard? I make a note to pick that one up once I get to that row. That's another reason the Jacksons probably like me. I always enjoy picking out the weird-shaped and discolored pumpkins. If I'm going to be baking with them it doesn't matter what they look like, and at the point I'm putting half a dozen or more on my porch as jack-o'-lanterns, why would I want them to all look "perfect"? That's boring.

I want the pumpkins to be as unique and full of character when I buy them as they are after I'm done with them. Their quirks inspire me on what to carve. I love it. I also always collect a copious amount of seeds after I finish and bake them. I tend to make enough to hand out little goodie bags of cinnamon spice pumpkin seeds to all my friends and coworkers. Maybe this year I should run a batch back out to the Jacksons. Definitely need some for April, Eric, Savannah, Damian...*fuck, Damian.*

That's a whole 'nother can of worms I have to figure out. He's handsome, charming, handy, and obviously flirting. But he's also a student, which as a lab assistant isn't *technically* forbidden, but it can be complicated. *I certainly couldn't grade any of his work...damn it, Celeste, why are you even trying to figure out the logistics?* I should *not* be entertaining this...

Sure, he's the first guy to make my heart flutter in years...well, the first real, *healthy*, option of a guy to do so. I roll my eyes at myself. *There's no hope for me.* But that doesn't mean I need to risk drama at work over my first attempt at being in a relationship again. Plus, am I even ready for that?

The image of him smiling down at me from on top of the ladder while he worked comes to mind. Those strange reddish hazel eyes melting me even when I'm just reliving the moment. I'd really like to see where this could go. He makes me laugh and blush. I get butterflies every time he shamelessly flirts. Talking to him was so easy and natural. Even Osiris seemed comfortable around him, which *never* happens. Animals can always sense things about people and I trust Osiris, he's a paranoid boy.

I figure that's why Issac never would let me get a pet, no matter how badly I wanted one. He always said he didn't think we were ready for that kind of responsibility, then it was about the extra pet fee for the apartment, and then it finally ended up boiling down to 'what if someone we want to host is allergic?' It was just *so inconsiderate* of me not to think of everyone else's possible needs before entertaining my own desires. But I think he knew deep down the animal wouldn't be able to bond with someone like him, and that would be the red flag I wouldn't ignore.

But Osiris was so calm around Damian immediately, when he even took time to warm up to April and Savannah. So there must be something great there that he's picking up on, right? Or am I looking for positives that aren't actually there like I did with Issac because I want this to be something good?

I spent years selling myself on all the "great" things about Issac while I was letting him tear me apart, piece by piece, until I didn't even recognize myself. How do you ever trust your interpretations of people after something like that? I'm clearly not a reliable narrator for myself, but I'm supposed to just move forward and find the right person while trusting I've made a good call? It's ludicrous.

Especially for a woman who just got turned on when she was jumped by a stalker in her house. That screams *great instincts.* The intended internal groan escapes me, so I quickly bend down to pick up a large pumpkin and pretend I was straining under the weight of it so I won't look like the crazy woman who is having a crisis of self in the middle of public like I currently am.

Doesn't matter if I like Damian or not, or if I even should. I have a feeling that the man who was in my house last night is not about to share me, and I shouldn't be putting anyone else at risk, even if I'm seriously considering leaving myself in danger for another taste of that thrill.

Damian

At first, I was happy to see she came here alone today, but I've been dwelling on why she's let me think she had an actual date since Wednesday if she didn't. Was she trying to give me a gentle brush off by implying she's already involved? Or was she trying to make me jealous? Perhaps pushing for me to make a move before it is more than just a casual date with someone?

Not knowing what she's thinking, even after watching her for months, drives me crazy. Being able to read people is how I survived as long as I did in my old career, it's a skill I pride myself on. But Celeste is hard to read in every way except her body. Now *that* I have come to understand very well.

My hands still tingle with excitement from getting to touch her last night. I spent most of the early morning hours sitting in the corn watching her after she sent me away. She didn't even leave her room. She laid right where I left her for the majority of the night, still staring into that mirror and thinking. I wanted so badly to go back and hold her, to let her talk her way through that internal struggle I knew she was dealing with, but I didn't think that would exactly go over well. So I just sat outside in the cold, ate every single caramel I had on me, and was there for her in the only way I could be.

Eventually, I went home to shower and get ready for today. But I was back, and waiting just inside the edge of the fields by her driveway, before the sun was fully up. My bike makes it easy to hide in the stalks and to catch up after letting her get far enough down the road for me to safely follow. I wasn't surprised when she came straight here, but I was intrigued when no one was waiting for her and she didn't seem to be expecting anyone else. She waved a greeting at the woman in the snack shack and jumped right into pulling some little wagon around the patch, collecting the oddest pumpkins of the bunch.

Jacksons' Farm is definitely a small, private family enterprise that seems like it is probably relying on the seasonal activity income just as much as its crops. I don't know if they have different types of public events, like that self-pick shit or whatever, the rest of the year, but they certainly built up under the expectation of entertaining families. They have a cleared dirt "parking lot" right beside a barn that has been renovated into a small store full of local honeys, homemade jams, and such products, a playground, a kiddie hayride, mini petting zoo, and snack shack that is surrounded by decorated picnic tables.

I decide to head over to the snack shack and buy something. The tables have a clear view of the pumpkin patch and my Sweet, but I need to look like I came out here for something other than the sights. I might get away with staring at a beautiful woman in general without raising any alarms, but a lone man in a hat and sunglasses doing nothing but sitting at a place where a ton of kids are running around barely supervised is going to draw attention.

The same older, grey-haired woman, that Celeste had waved to earlier, greets me at the window with a warm smile. I quickly scan the menu, which is filled with all sorts of pumpkin, cinnamon, apple, and pecan flavored versions of diabetes. *Damn, between this and the caramels, Celeste isn't even going to need a knife to kill me.* My eyes flick back over my shoulder to where she's meandering through the patch, clearly lost in thought. She looks like a daydream in this festive little sundress she has on. A halter top number that cinches in at the waist and goes out into a flowy skirt that dances between her legs as she walks. It's black with little ghosts printed all over it. The way she smiles with patience when two kids cut in front of her while pulling a little wagon in that dress - I can so easily picture our children running around here like all these other kids until she calls them back and they come running just to wrap themselves around her in a hug.

"Spiced apple cider is her favorite."

I jolt and whip back around to be met with an amused, knowing smile on the old lady's face, "Excuse me?"

"The young lady in the black dress? Her favorite drink is spiced apple cider, she's also fond of the pumpkin funnel cake. You know, in case you were wondering."

"Oh, uh, no thanks. I'll just take a black coffee and a slice of the pecan pie."

She sucks her teeth at me, inspecting me critically. "Your loss. That one's sweet, pretty, and won't be on the market long." She spins on her heels to collect my order, mumbling grumpily to herself about dumbass little boys not knowing a good girl when they see one.

I can't help but smile. If she only knew exactly how sold I was on Celeste at first sight and what I've been up to because of it she might rethink her attitude about how men should be paying attention to good girls. But when she returns and I pay for my food, I leave her with an extra twenty to cover whatever treat Celeste might decide she wants. I'll be headed out as soon as she's done in the patch; I can't risk her seeing me.

The old lady smiles, looking at me like she knows more than she should, as I take my snacks to a table to savor watching the only Sweet I really want, enjoy herself. Her wagon is already almost full, a complete menagerie of various shaped and colored pumpkins. Like a kid who was let loose in a candy store, she has grabbed every one that has caught her eye. But that joy hasn't reached them.

Her eyes seem far off, still lost in that inner struggle with who she thinks she should be versus that immaculate creature she actually is. I can't deny that I planned to execute last night when I did so that I would be heavy on her mind while she was out on this "date" with someone else. I *needed* to be her focus no matter who had her actual company, but what I *did* to her? *That* was specifically designed to make her face herself. I can see the beauty in her twisted darkness, just like she sees it in her oddities, but she needs to see it herself. She and I, *we*, and exactly what our future looks like depends on her acceptance of all sides of herself.

Celeste

Five days and nights have passed, and I still haven't told anyone what happened. I've worked with Savannah every night since Sunday and I haven't said a thing. I could've called April anytime and she would've picked up, but I haven't. Hell, there's a counselor on campus I could've gone and talked to...though they'd have probably had me committed. *Is this some convoluted form of selfharm?*

I'm nearing my house as I ponder that loaded question. I just wrapped up my last shift for the week and I'm about to be home alone for the next two days. Normally, I'd spend this time finishing decorating the house, carving the rest of the pumpkins, and cleaning the yard for the annual movie under-the-stars party coming up next week, but I can't help but wonder if I'll have the chance. If he's followed me for this long, then I'm sure he knows my schedule. He's just as aware of the fact that I'm unexpected for the next sixty hours as I am.

The way my thighs tighten instinctually at that mere thought is why I haven't said anything. I *know* this is crazy and dangerous. I *know* I should tell someone. I *know* I should not go back to this house alone for the next two days. But then all of this could end and as much as I can't give myself one goddamn logical reason why, I don't *want* it to end. This demented pumpkin is like a virus that has invaded my system, making me feverish and delirious, probably bad for my health yet I just can't shake him. *But is this a terminal diagnosis?*

The girls love me, but I don't think they would understand. Savannah might try to talk sense into me and then tell me it's my choice but April would never leave me alone again. She might even try to have me deemed mentally unstable if I fought her on it. *She may be right, but that's not the point.* At least, I hope that's how it would go. Part of me fears they'd judge me and never want anything to do with me again. Like I'm some screwed up deviant who is an affront to all women because I have reactions I shouldn't to things that are royally fucked. The exact same kinds of reactions I know my family and Issac would have to me.

But no matter if they understood it or not, with all that is happening in my life at the moment, I know I would never excuse the sexual assault of anyone, man or woman. It's horrific and reprehensible. No one is ever asking for it unless they use their actual voice to express consent and a desire for it. This stalker assaulted me because he didn't get consent and that's not okay...*but between me and myself, I know I want it.* My *real* problem is that I don't know how to handle the fact that I *do* want the scary, masked man to make me tremble again... *What kind of woman does that make me?*

I can see my house much clearer tonight as I pull into the driveway. The moon is waxing and almost back up to the first quarter again. *Has it already been almost a month? I guess time flies by when your days are filled with a stalker, mental chaos, and identity crises.* I snatch my bag up and head to the porch, stepping around the elaborate arrangement of unlit jack-o'-lanterns, trying to decide what movie Osiris and I are going to unwind to, because I'm way too worked up to go straight to sleep. *Something campy, like* Zombie Strippers *or* House of a 1000 Corpses. I unlock the door and walk in, calling out to Osiris as I turn on lights throughout the house.

He comes trudging out of the theatre, like he was already expecting it to be a movie night. I pop open a can of wet food for him to enjoy while I slip into the bathroom and get comfortable. About ten minutes later, I emerge in nothing but a giant ratty t-shirt, with all my makeup wiped off, and my hair pushed back in a headband.

"Come on, boy, let's go watch some blonde, big titty girls get torn apart." I pick Osiris up, petting him as we head to the theatre.

He looks up at me, tilting his head with a sass that seems to say, 'Bitch, like you might not end up being one of those girls?'

"Shut up," I snap at the cat who didn't actually say anything, but we both know he meant it.

I ended up deciding to go with the *My Bloody Valentine* remake that was originally a 3D movie release and has all the delightfully crappy in your face 'coming right at you' camera shots. But when I go to pop the disc in, *Darkness Falls* is sitting in the tray.

I haven't watched this in forever. Is this maniac really just watching movies in my house? What the fuck? Why would he do that? *Good taste though, that movie is an underrated classic.* Celeste! *For fuck's sake that's not what is important right now.* I calmly take the disc out and put it back in its case on the shelf. Fuck him. He wants to scare me. That's what's getting him off. I don't know if he's watching me right now or not, but I'm not going to give him the satisfaction. I'm not scared and I don't give a damn if he's been here today.

I take my seat, curl up with Osiris, and start the movie like nothing was out of the ordinary. But I really didn't expect to somehow be so comfortable that I'd fall asleep on the recliner in the first half hour of the movie.

Damian

I lost track of time watching the movie with Osiris and barely got the TV turned off before she was coming through the door. I'm so glad her driveway is gravel. I hid in the theatre while she fed the cat and then I slipped down to her bedroom when she was in the bathroom. I put the mask on and was waiting for her to come to bed when I heard her tell Osiris that they had movie plans.

My mind immediately went to the disc I had left in the player. *Shit. It's okay, I can still work with this. I'll wait right in the doorway and when she makes a break for the front door I'll grab her.* I positioned myself and waited. For five minutes, then ten, and then suddenly I could hear the screams from a movie. *What? She had to have noticed.*

I creep down the hall. She turned on all the lights along the main path through the house, so I have nothing to help hide me. I stay low and close to the wall, trying to keep my shadow from being too noticeable. The door to the theatre is cracked and I peek through to see just the top edge of her head over the back of the chair. The way it is tilted, I'd assume she's leaning on her propped up arm, legs curled up under her with Osiris on her lap. Her typical, adorable movie watching pose. The mental image brings a smile to my face.

I've watched her in this position countless times through the cameras, but I've never been this close...this intimate with her...in moments like this. *My plans can wait a little bit, I am not about to pass this up.* Even though I am not able to touch her, there's something peaceful about just sitting in her presence while she simply *exists*. Celeste is my heaven, here for me to taste on earth, since I certainly won't be going there when I die.

I spend the next twenty minutes or so watching her and the movie through the crack, when suddenly her small snores carry across the room. I know it is stupid and risky, but I can't resist. I push the door open slowly, just far enough that I can slip in and then carefully slide it back behind me. Timidly, I move across the dim room, only lit by the movie, until I'm standing at the end of the recliners.

She's curled up in the chair farthest from me, in the exact position I pictured. Osiris lifts his head to appraise me, purrs, and lays back down on her. The light of the movie illuminates her stunning face in an eerie blue hue, one I'm sure she'd appreciate if she could see it. The desire to kiss her surges through me, so I pop a caramel into my mouth to stave off the temptation. *Damn, she's too fucking pretty for either of our sakes.* I don't know what I'm thinking, *actually I'm not thinking at all,* but I sit down in the other recliner. I just *need* this moment with her. More than the chemistry, the lust, the passion...I need the peace she brings me.

In moments like this, none of my demons or nightmares can reach me. She is my sanctuary. I will never outrun who I am inside, but with her, it feels like that person is someone I can live with being. My whole life my mother told me I was a demon, whether the world saw it yet or not. She beat it into me until I decided to be exactly what I was meant to be. But no matter how much blood I coated myself in, I still never felt like I had quite matched the beast inside. But what Celeste brings out in me, that balance of violence and pleasure feels like home. *I feel whole.*

I'm going to watch the rest of the movie like this, wrapped up in her and the energy between us. But once it ends, it is game on my Sweet.

Celeste

I startle awake to a loud sound. Jerking upright so hard that I knock Osiris off my lap, only for him to hiss his disapproval before he trots out of the room, pushing the door open to a dark hallway.

I left that light on. I know I did.

I look over at the TV and the DVD selection screen is playing on repeat, its low suspenseful music on a loop. Below it, the clock says it's just past five in the morning. *It's just a hall light Celeste, don't jump to conclusions.* But in my gut I fucking *know* I left that light on. My hand starts to shake but I can't honestly tell if it is more from fear or excitement. *Knife. Now.*

If he's waiting for me, then there's no point to sneaking around, it isn't going to accomplish anything. He already knows I'm in the house. So then I'll go in fast, hard, and bold.

Surprise him and throw him off his game in a different way. *Good plan. Now, fucking do it.* I breathe deep before I throw open the theatre room's door, swing around the frame, and start sprinting down the hall to get a knife.

But I skid to a stop, almost tumbling forward over myself, as I skitter into the middle of the kitchen when I see his shadowy figure sitting up on my counter in the dark, twirling a knife back and forth between his hands. It's hard to make out in the dim light, but the knife is large. The blade is smooth along most of the length, with serrations beginning about two inches from the tactical looking handle. The metal keeps catching the minimal light and flashing in the dark as he *plays* with it. He is shirtless, with only the shawled pumpkin mask, gloves, black jeans, and boots on. It's too dark to make out the details, but his sculpted chest and entire stomach is covered in tattoos. His inhumanely deep voice echoes as he says, "Oh fun, my Sweet is *finally* awake."

I can hear the smug chuckle and grin he's hiding behind that mask. Taunting me with the fact that he was in here while I was asleep. That he could've killed me before I even knew what was coming. But we both know better because he clearly needs me awake, he craves my interaction and attention too much to just finish me off while I'm asleep.

He wants fear. *Fuck him.*

"Well it's five in the morning and I didn't invite you over, so excuse me if I don't feel guilty about not being the best host."

He doesn't move from his hunched over perch on my counter, but the knife goes still. The pumpkin mask staring back at me in the gloom like some creature from my deepest, darkest, most delicious nightmares.

"Does it seem like I need an invitation?"

I huff, and with either bravery or stupidity, I turn my back on him and head over to the fridge. I can feel his gaze burning into me while I grab a Cheerwine. Spinning around, I look at him as I pop the tab and let the hiss of the carbonation cut the thick silence.

"You don't seem to think you need one, but your lack of manners doesn't entitle you to my hospitality." I take a sip. "So, since I don't plan to offer you a refreshment, and I'd *really* like to go back to bed, I'd suggest you find your way out of my house before I finish my drink. You clearly know where the front door is since you keep letting yourself in."

I cross my arms and lean back against the fridge as I sip on the soda and stare him down. But the sound of his cold, hollow laugh in that eerie voice changer sends chills down my body that I pray the darkness is able to hide from him.

"Well, well. Look who is standing up to the villain with the big knife." He jumps off the counter, the weight of his massive body making the floor bounce with the impact. He straightens, rolling his shoulders as he twists his wrist and points the knife at me. "Now, Celeste, we both know that means one of two things for you."

"Oh yeah, and what's that, pumpkin face?"

The ice in his response makes my heart drop into my stomach. "You either end up the iconic final girl or in pieces of the pretty big titty blonde whose name no one ever remembers." He turns to face me fully, but doesn't step closer.

Fuck. I was right and now I've pissed him off.

"I'm not afraid of you."

Oh yeah, that's gonna help.

But as much as my inner voice wants to judge me for being dumb, my pride is louder. If this motherfucker is going to kill me, then I'm at least going to stick it to him as much as I can. Killing me isn't going to be satisfying. I'm going to the grave as annoying as fucking possible.

"Is that so?" His low, even reply sounds more like a challenge than a question.

I take another sip of my drink like a soda is gonna give me some kind of liquid courage. *Nope. This has got to be all you girl.* "Why should I be? You keep sneaking in and out of my house at all hours of the night like a field mouse seeking shelter from the real predators out there. A nuisance? Sure. But nothing to fear."

His grip on the knife tightens. Even in the darkness, I can see his knuckles straining the leather of his gloves. "Oh, my Sweet, I've clearly been *far* too gentle if you think I'm not the predator that stalks the fields outside your house at night...let me correct that for you."

I swear to God the air around us drops ten degrees as he exhales. My bravado is wavering but I refuse to let him win. I huff, roll my eyes, and start to walk back to the hallway. Trying to keep an air of nonchalance despite the rocks settling into the pit of my stomach.

But the moment I reach the mouth of the hall, he takes one step behind me and my entire nervous system goes haywire. Adrenaline floods my veins and my flight instincts kick into high gear. As soon as I hear his footfall connect with the linoleum, I drop the drink and am running full speed towards my front door.

He must have expected it though because he is right on my heels. *I swear I can feel the heat of his breath on my neck, he's so close.* My house is small, I have mere seconds to make a plan. I realize I won't have time to open the front door fully but a window would take even longer. Maybe I can jerk it open into him and stun him long enough to make a break for it.

At this point I'm just steps from the front door, fully committed to destroying his nose with it, when he turns up the speed and slides past me, swinging the knife. It slices through the air right in front of me before it sinks into the wall, his arm barring my path. I scream, the piercing sound carrying through the house and out into the night, but I know there's no one to hear me. *No one is coming.* I grab onto the wall as I try to stop myself from colliding into him, but my momentum tangles my feet, making me stumble and topple over.

Goddamn it, Celeste, did you really just trip over air while running from the killer? Typical. Karma's a bitch, I'm about to die just like all the characters I used to mock. GREAT. Instinctually, I lean back from him, slowly scooting myself away as he pulls the knife from the drywall, never breaking his gaze with me. A small shower of plaster and paint fall through the air as the blade comes free.

He waves the knife back and forth, as if chastising me. "Really? Sweet, you know better than to trip, that's not going to help you at all." He tosses the knife up in the air, letting it flip before he expertly catches it by the handle again.

My pulse is racing so fast, it feels like my blood vessels might burst from the pressure. All logical thought is lost at this point. There is nothing but an instinct to flee and that's exactly what I attempt to do. Flipping over and scrambling to my feet, I make a run for my bedroom and try to slam the door shut behind me. He slides his shoulder and thigh into the door frame and eats the impact. I don't even hear a groan of pain or discomfort.

I'm leaning back on it with every ounce of my weight, feet planted and applying pressure. But all I can do is watch in horror as his hand that's inside the room reaches up to grab the edge of the door, his other slipping into view as if in slow motion to do the same. With a grunt, he pushes against it.

My feet slip one inch, then another. I scream in desperation as I push back harder, convinced the door might break off its hinges, but it's no use. He shoves again and the sudden force breaks all my traction, launching me off the door and forward into my nightstand. It slams open, banging into the wall without the resistance. I look back over my shoulder to face an image that is straight from all of my most depraved dreams...*good and bad.*

The moonlight is streaming in from the window, illuminating him in the doorway. He fills the space, his massive shoulders and build making my place look more like a dollhouse. That same twisted mask staring down at me, never blinking, never revealing any emotions or thoughts. The ink across his chest and stomach appears to be intricate black and grey imagery of heaven and hell at war, various angels and demons locked in battles. The closer I look, the more I can make out the details. The angels are losing every single conflict. *Is that how he sees his mind? His soul?*

His body is heaving just slightly with the exertion from our battle with the door. Moonlight glistens off a bead of sweat that rolls down his chest from under the edge of the mask. The image of catching it on the tip of my tongue and licking up the path flashes through my mind. *Celeste! What the* fuck?! His fingers stretch and readjust over the handle of the knife.

There's nowhere to go. I turn and face him, backed up against my night stand. *Go to the grave as annoying as possible bitch.* "So what now pumpkin face? Pillow fight?"

He's across the room and grabbing up a fistful of my oversized t-shirt before I can even register it. Jerking hard, he tosses me sideways onto the bed and slams the knife into the mattress in the gap between my thighs as soon as I land.

I squeal, my stomach knotting and my thighs flying open wider to run from the threat. His rumbling snicker invades the ring of my scream. "I don't know if I'd suggest bringing a pillow to a knife fight."

Suddenly the knife is back out, flashing through the air, before it slams into the pillow beside my head. I can't help it, I jump again. He slides himself over me. My body pulls away from the blade, forcing me to writhe against him as I move. My breasts are pressing into his chest as my back and hips roll beneath him. I hear the smallest tease of a groan escape his lips as I press myself against his pants.

He moves to place one of his legs on either side of my thighs, sitting up and pinning mine. Lifting the knife, he brings the pillow with it. He rips it off without looking away from me, raining down stuffing on top of us as he tosses it aside. I can't bring myself to break our stare, but from the corner of my eye, I catch a glimpse of a lone tattoo on his forearm. A classic pin-up witch sitting on a pumpkin. *Does she look like...me?*

The mask moves slightly as his gaze slithers down my body. It only takes this single moment of stillness for me to register that I am *soaking* wet. My thighs are slick with my arousal.

In a voice so low, I'm not sure I was meant to hear it, he says, "Fuck, you are magnificent." And despite everything that is happening, that brings a light blush to my cheeks that I hope he can't see.

Louder and with a growl that is dripping sin, he adds, "You writhe so prettily, my Sweet, but I want to appreciate the whole view." His hand brushes over my shirt, crunching it up as he goes. It exposes my mound with a small tuft of hair and the bottom of my soft stomach, but he doesn't seem satisfied. As he reaches the top, he suddenly grabs it by the neck and jerks up, lifting my back off the bed, and letting my head fall.

"Do. Not. Move." He barks and I freeze without question, locked in an arch, up on my elbows to hold the position, and head tilted back watching him upside down in my closet mirror. He brings the knife to the edge of the neckline and tugs hard, pulling the shirt up and the blade down to cut through the fabric quickly. I suck my stomach in instinctually, but he doesn't graze me.

He sits up, looking into the mirror to meet the reflection of my eyes with those soulless black voids as he releases the fabric, letting it fall open over my bare flesh. The leather of his glove is warm with his body heat as he runs it slowly from the base of my throat, between the valley of my breasts, and over my stomach to stop just above my mound. I shiver deliciously as I watch him in the mirror. Almost like I'm witnessing it happen to an actress so I don't have to make excuses for why my sheets are moist beneath me, I can just watch it like I do my slashers and enjoy the show guilt free.

Suddenly, he presses into my torso, breaking my form and laying me flat on the bed. My eyes fly to the mirrors on the ceiling, seeking that sanctuary. I'm staring at my own reflection, admiring the way my body is posed out on the sheets and the way the flush has spread on my skin like I would any other scream queen, when he growls, "Now writhe for me, my Sweet."

The knife is slammed into the bed just off my hip making me jerk away. He does it again, and again, and again off of different parts of my body. My torso slides over the silk sheets easily, but the soaked ones beneath my thighs stick to my skin. I can feel his eyes burning into me as he savors the way he can make me jump, squeal, and scream as my body dances from his blade. But my eyes stay glued to those mirrors and I watch the star he is making of me. *God, it is so erotic.*

My bed is being skewered, but I can't find it in me to care at this moment. He has me worked up into a tizzy, the adrenaline and fear are clearly an addictive combination to my libido. *I swear a single touch would make me spasm in orgasm at this point.* I lose count of how many times he slams the knife down, but finally he takes my chin in his hand and gently pulls it down, so that I meet his masked gaze.

My chest is heaving with rapid shallow breaths and my throat is sore from screaming, but I can't help but smile when I look at him. His hand slides gently over my cheek to the back of my head, until it locks into my hair and takes control. Pulling hard enough to keep my attention but not to truly hurt me.

"You are lucky that you are too damn pretty to die yet. Maybe you do have final girl potential, my Sweet. But don't ever forget that I am the predator that stalks the fields outside your home, I just like playing with my food first."

I gasp as his hand slips between my legs. The knife handle does one quick glide along my dripping slit, grinding against my clit *just right* to set me off. My hands snatch up the tattered sheets, as my back arches, and I choke out my moan, simultaneously forgetting how to breathe. The most intense orgasm of my life is wracking my body and I swear my vision flashes white during it. I'm absolutely lost in the throws of my pleasure. It leaves me panting, gasping, and dripping sweat.

It actually takes me a moment to realize that my eyes are still closed as I'm simply lying there, comfortably satisfied, in the presence of a psycho stalker that I just let get me off while scaring me with a *fucking knife.*

At least I thought I was. But when I force myself to open my eyes and face what just happened, I also become aware of the lack of body weight and heat on top of me. I sit up in my ruined bed only to find a silent, empty room. If it wasn't for the eviscerated sheets and mattress, I might believe I was actually starting to lose my mind.

Celeste

It's kinda slow for a Saturday. I groan. Terrible timing considering I'm now in need of a new mattress and sheets. I tossed a framed picture up over the hole in my wall by the front door, but the bed isn't such an easy fix. *Motherfucker, thinking he's all* BIG *and* BAD. *We will see how bad he thinks he is after I poke as many holes in him as he poked in my bed.* That's all I've been allowing myself to ponder today - how irritated I am at the destruction and how satisfying it would be to stab him.

I won't...*can't*...allow myself to focus on how my body reacted to the fear and excitement. How it responded to *him*. How I never even *considered* saying "trick." I had to go to work tonight, and every time this week that I've tried to process what happened Wednesday, I've ended up a fucking mess. Because I'm either unable to deal with my guilt over my depravity or I'm unable to stop with the *self-gratification* in response to it. Thus, there was no time for reflection over the absolute debauchery of this week if I was going to be able to function for work.

At least it's steady enough to keep my mind from wandering too far, even if it isn't looking like I'll be getting that new mattress anytime soon. *Complaining like you didn't force a dildo down into one of the rips and then ride it to three orgasms last night, reliving what happened.* Shit. Clearly not steady *enough.* But while I'm chastising myself for my delightfully whorish, but absolutely unhinged behavior, the door chimes announcing the arrival of a new guest.

I'm in the middle of a draft pour, so I call out my typical, "Welcome to Juke's!" greeting, only to spill a little when I hear a very familiar voice reply his thanks as he slides into a seat at the bar.

Damian.

"Oh, well hi, you," I'm blushing, I can feel the heat on my cheeks as I clean the glass and pass the beer to the customer, before I turn to meet those pretty reddish eyes and that devilish grin. "Here for that 'thank you' drink?"

He is emanating joy, glowing from the inside out. I don't know what's gotten into him, but I like it. It's nice to see anyone *that* happy, but especially him...I brush off the sudden intrusive question of *why* 'especially him'. *Nope. That's definitely another problem to tackle on a day I don't have to function.*

"What can I get you?"

He hums as he considers for a moment. "How about a rum and coke? And yes, I *will* take whatever quality of liquor you use as a sign of exactly how happy you are with my service." His voice drops a touch as he says 'service'. That, along with his sexy, sinful smirk, makes my mind flash with a whole reel of how his double entendre could come to life. *Fuck, Celeste. How goddamn horny are you? Get yourself together.*

I make a show of grabbing Captain Morgan off the bottom shelf and setting it on the bar, enjoying the mock offense on his face. But after I pick out a fresh glass, I take the Brugal 1888 from our top shelf to make his drink.

"Oh, now *that* looks nice."

Laughing, I slide it to him and return the bottles to their places as I wait for him to taste it. But his small moan of satisfaction slips out while I have my back turned and I can't help but shiver with the chill that runs down my spine. *Holy fuck, that was hot.*

"Sounds like you're enjoying yourself back there," I call over my shoulder. I definitely need another moment to catch my breath before I turn and face him after that, so I start wiping down the back counter to buy time.

"Well I've got a stunning view while sipping on an excellent drink that's on a pretty bartender's tab, why wouldn't I be enjoying myself?"

I laugh as I spin to face him, in shock and disbelief. *He's so bold. But so respectful and charming at the same time. He's dangerous to my heart...but am I dangerous to him?* I'd hate for him to get caught in the middle of this stalker mess just because

I'm too selfish to send him away when I know I should. Getting butterflies when he smiles at me is not enough of a reason to put this poor man at risk.

"Shitttt, do you plan to give free drinks and show off your ass to all of us? Sign me up. I'd have come here sooner if I knew the bartenders were slutty." Some louse towards the other end of my bar is leaning over the counter, hands wrapped around the edge with his head and shoulders hanging off, leering at me with a yellow gap-toothed grin. He isn't one of my regulars.

I grab the dispenser nozzle and all of my actual regulars lean back in their seats because they know what's coming. I take one step, aim, and spray the man in the face with water as he sputters and slaps at the stream pathetically, his legs kicking on the other side of the bar.

"Cold showers are twenty dollars. You can pay it into the tip jar and continue to drink, or you can leave my establishment for non-payment of services. Pick." I squirt one more quick shot of water at him, making him jump as I drive home my point.

His wet, scraggly, thinning hair hangs down in his face, which is puffy and flushed with rage, "You bitch," he bites out as he suddenly swings his legs around and pops over the bar. "Who the fuck do you think you are? I'll fucking show you, whore."

He's storming down the backside of the bar towards me. Patrons are calling out my name and I hear one particular woman scream for someone to call the police, but I'm too busy backing up as fast as I can to pay any attention to them. We keep a bat hidden under the end of the bar that's behind me. I can't bring myself to turn my back on him though, so I'm stumbling, flashes of Issac's face twisted in that same rage making my blood run cold.

But right as I bump into the counter's edge and go to reach for the bat, I blink and he's gone. It takes me a second to register that as the asshole passed Damian, he was snatched up by his shirt, dragged back over the bar, and tossed halfway across the place. Damian is on top of him, pummeling into the creep over and over. Crimson already painting them both.

"Damian! Stop!"

His fist stalls in the air, still poised for another blow. He doesn't look back at me, but I can see a slight tremble in his body as he breathes deep, sits up on the asshole, and runs his messy hands through his hair as he collects himself, streaking it with blood. Standing slowly, he gets off the man and then lifts him to his feet, not paying any attention to the silent crowd watching.

The drunk looks dazed, but alive. Blood is pouring from a broken nose and busted mouth, but I don't see any new missing teeth. Damian doesn't give the man a chance to process what happened or who is escorting him out. He basically drags him from the bar, disappearing out the doors with him. A few patrons follow, probably to be sure the conflict doesn't resume...*or to watch if it does.* But Damian returns, without the jackass, just a minute later.

The bar is still quiet, other than the radio playing in the background. Though as he takes his seat again the murmurs pick up and in mere moments the energy is back in full swing as if nothing happened. That's one thing about being in the country versus California. If no one needed a hospital after a bar fight, and it was one-on-one and hand-to-hand, then it was fair and nothing comes of it.

I pass Damian a fresh, wet towel and a rag full of ice. "You didn't have to do that. I have a bat hidden under the bar. But thank you anyway."

He wipes his hands and knuckles clean of the blood. They're busted and raw, a little swollen from the injuries. *Shit, maybe I should've counted the guy's teeth twice.* Instinctually, I look back at the floor behind Damian to see if there is any yellow debris lying around, but the dishwasher is already out there cleaning up the mess. *Damn, guess I'll never know...maybe I shouldn't worry so much about the stalker. Clearly, Damian can handle his own.*

He pushes the ice back towards me, politely refusing it. While staring down at his hands, flexing them, testing the wounds, he replies, "It wouldn't mean anything if I had to do it. It's choices that define us, not requirements." The last part came out automatic, like it's something he's said many times.

I pick up the rag and take both of his fists into one of my open palms and press the ice to them with my other hand. His beautiful reddish hazel eyes lift to stare at my face as I tend to him. "True, which means you *chose* to intervene. That means even more." I look up to meet his gaze.

His eyes look heavy with the weight of something, all that infectious light and joy from earlier gone. My chest stings with the loss of that glow. *No.*

"Which is why I'd appreciate it if you'd join me for a bite to eat after work."

His eyebrow quirks sarcastically, "At like, what? Two in the morning?"

"I have to eat sometime. All-night diners were made for third shift workers, didn't you know?" I smile at him, hoping that I can give him a touch of that happiness back.

His eyes are searching mine desperately, with a look I recognize. He's been hurt before. Kindness feels like a trap, and he's hesitant to trust it, but...he wants to. Finally he says, "You don't have to do that."

I pause, making sure to stare into his heart and soul as I say this, needing him to feel the force behind each word. "If I had to, it wouldn't mean anything."

Damian

The harsh lights reflecting off the bleached tiles of this diner are a drastic contrast to the darkness outside the huge windows. I have to admit, this is not where I envisioned our first date, but I also never imagined she'd be the one asking me out either. *And I am not about to complain.*

Is this a date though? Or am I just jumping to conclusions? This is certainly not how I saw the night going. I wasn't planning to ever really take her up on that free drink, but after watching her escapades over the last couple days, I couldn't stay away. I'm surprised I haven't put on ten pounds in nothing but caramels.

I've been glued to the cameras, even at work. I kept making up reasons to be on my phone so I could watch her as she blossomed into that dark, divine creature she truly is. It'll take time for her mind to fully accept it, but her body is already sold. She has spent days playing with herself, reliving our game just like I have, and her flesh knows this is what she craves.

The way she challenged me that night, even when facing down possible death, was thrilling. My Sweet has a bitter, bratty streak and I love it. That heat and spark just adds to the raging inferno of desire I already have for her. I love that she pushes back at me just as much as I'm pushing at her limits.

I know the more I mingle with her as myself, the more I risk my carefully made plans, but I can't help it. I need to be near her. So after I dropped off her first quarter moon gift, a new mattress and sheets, I came to Juke's to have a drink, flirt, and go home with the scent of her perfume fresh in my mind...*Now I'm sitting in a diner on a date? I'm not fucking prepared for this.*

I didn't need to be prepared to beat the shit out of that asshole earlier. That comes naturally. *Instinctually.* The way his face cracked beneath my fist was familiar, *normal.* Hell, I clocked his license plate so I could finish his lesson later without even thinking about it. But being alone with this sweet, charming witch without fumbling and blowing my cover? That I *definitely* needed to prepare for. *I'm so fucked.*

I watch as she makes her way back from the bathroom, with an effervescent smile on her face that melts me. Something I never would've thought was possible a year ago, but here I am, a puddle in a cheap, squeaky, vinyl booth. This little spellcaster has me wrapped around her finger and she doesn't even know it. *And there's nowhere else I'd rather be.*

The way she didn't retreat from me after she saw what lurks behind that wall that I dedicate so much energy to maintaining surprised me...and gave me hope that maybe we aren't so far from the day that she accepts us for what we are meant to be together. There was something in her eyes when she said "If I had to, it wouldn't mean anything," that made it clear she is feeling the same pull that I am. Maybe not as extreme, or maybe she just hasn't given into her inner psycho as much, but she feels that magnetism.

She slides into the seat across from me and passes me a menu without taking one for herself. "Do you already know what you want?"

Her cheeks flush and she brushes her hair behind her ears like she always does when she's embarrassed. "Yeah...it's September so the seasonal stuff has started. For the next two months, you won't catch me ordering anything but cinnamon baked apple french toast here."

Figures. "Hmm, sounds...*interesting.*" I glance over the menu, not really giving a damn about what I'm going to eat, but also trying to appear *somewhat* normal.

"It's better than it sounds! You'll have to try a bite when it comes out," she declares, dramatically lifting her chin as if a queen who has made a declaration. *I wouldn't dare argue, my Sweet.*

"Oh this looks festive as well." I notice a pumpkin pancake with powdered sugar on it and think back to the old woman at the patch's snack shack telling me how Celeste loved the funnel cakes. This should be pretty close. "I think I'm going to try the sugar and spice pumpkin pancakes."

Her eyes widen in wonder. "Those must be new."

"Well, you'll have to try a bite when it comes out," I smirk. "I insist."

She laughs, the most beautiful sound in the world. Between her laughs and her screams, I won't ever have a need for music again.

We order and eat pretty quickly, but we sit there until after five in the morning talking. It's so easy with her. Never in my life have I wanted to talk to someone so much. I don't share a lot because I can't afford to slip up and reveal something vital, but I could listen to her forever; about California, college, Ammerton, her friends, Osiris, movies, *anything*. But when she yawns, I know that she needs her rest. Plus, she has a nice new mattress waiting for her to break it in and I'm anxious to watch.

"Seems like sleep might be calling you away from me."

She smiles apologetically. "I'm sorry. I have had a blast, I just haven't been getting enough rest lately."

I'm aware. "Oh, nothing too serious, I hope?"

She sputters for a moment, but slides her smile back into place in a mere second. *Quick. She's used to having to hide her feelings.*

"No, nothing serious. Just too wrapped up in home projects and spooky season stuff. Been staying up too late watching scary movies." She shrugs her shoulders with her hands out to either side. *Adorable and very good at hiding those feelings.*

"Well let's get you home, Ms. Carroll," I wink, enjoying the blush it brings out. I pull out enough to cover the entire tab and lay it on the table. She starts to object but I simply shake my head in response. "I insist." I offer her my hand and help her from the booth.

We head outside and I open her car door for her. She pauses as she gets in, looking up at me over the frame between us. As often as I wish I could read her mind, I don't need a superpower to do it right now, because I know we are both having the same thought. *Was this date? Should we kiss? What now?*

I am craving to taste her again like an addict jonesing for a hit, but I don't want our next kiss to be unsure, timid, or in a parking lot right before we head different ways. So I resolve myself, "Goodnight, Celeste, I will see you in class on Tuesday."

The flash of disappointment in her eyes guts me and I almost fold right then and there. But she puts that expert mask on again in a flash, giving me a sweet smile as she waves. "Goodnight, Damian, drive safe. See you in class."

I stand in the parking lot, chewing a caramel as I watch her pull out and disappear down the road. Her emotional masks look an awful lot like my inner walls. Maybe the witch and the demon share more than just sexual predilections.

Damian

Waiting until Tuesday to see her in person was excruciating, but I managed. *It's a damn good thing I have such great self control, or else this entire plan would've been out the window by now.* I kept myself busy Sunday night by cruising the other bars in town until I came across that sleazy lowlife's car. I waited for him to leave and followed him home, *just* to make sure he understood never to come to Juke's again. But I made my point clear by taking a couple teeth with me that I intend to make into some weird oddity art for Celeste's collection. I'm sure I'll tell her where they came from...one day.

But that still left last night. I fought off the urge to go over and have a movie night with Osiris. I've done it successfully a hundred times during the last year, but ever since this game started, it has become harder and harder to leave without seeing her first. So I decided to go swing by Sam's and get him off my back.

I went by to see him last month when he asked, but it was barely what you could call a visit. We got into it over Kage pretty quickly and I left. I know I've been acting odd and distant because *I am* up to something, but it's not related to

Kage and his presumption that I'd just follow him back into that life pissed me off. But in the weeks since, in the *very few* moments I've not been consumed by Celeste, my mind has drifted to Sam.

I won't...no, I can't tell him what I've been up to. He wouldn't understand, hell he may even fear for Celeste because he thinks I've cracked. He's a good man like that. But there's no denying I've been acting suspicious and dodging him, which I've never done before, so of course he has every logical reason to believe I'd "fallen off the wagon". So I went over last night with a pizza and a fifth of whiskey to make peace.

The guilt hit a little harder when he greeted me at the door like the prodigal son, with relief on his face and arms open wide before I even had a chance to retrieve the olive branches from the truck. We spent a few hours together. I tried to talk as openly as I could to assuage his fears without revealing too much. It's difficult not being completely forthcoming with Sam. He's the closest thing I have to a friend and a mentor. He went through hell and back getting me out of the LaCroix family business. I owe him the last ten years of my life. *I owe him this chance at a future with Celeste.*

So I shared with him I had met someone and that it was serious, which he had assumed due to the tattoo. But I told him that I hadn't been able to tell her about myself and my past yet and I was trying to keep her away from anyone or anything that's related to it until I get the chance to be forthcoming with her. He was elated for me. Absolutely over the moon. Sam told me to man up and tell her before Christmas because he wanted to meet her by the holidays, after listening to me talk about her for almost an hour.

It was...*nice* to talk about Celeste that way. Like a normal man talks about his woman. She's amazing and deserves the praise, but it's kinda hard to brag about a woman you're stalking.

He did ask me about Kage, but he believed me when I told him that I hadn't heard from him until he ambushed me in the tattoo shop. Sam also agreed that it certainly isn't going to be another ten years till I see him again. Kage LaCroix isn't one to settle for less than everything he wants. He doesn't believe in compromise. It's served him well apparently, but he knows better than to try to play that hand with me. He really should be a smarter gambler than that by now. My own blood or not, I'll spill it all the same. I've done it before.

Once Sam seemed satisfied, either because of my answers or his fourth whiskey on the rocks, I left. Going back to my apartment instead of Celeste's house was a herculean task, but I managed to spend the night simply watching the cameras, chewing caramels, and planning our next game. Well, that and jerking off twice to the recordings from this past week. Between our chase and game and how she played with herself for the days after, I won't ever need internet porn again. *That woman really is a witch, and I am completely under her spell.*

Lab couldn't come fast enough. I was on campus an hour early, anxious to see her. It was ridiculous. *I'm acting like a fucking school boy.* But as much as I don't understand it, and I *want* to hate it, I can't. How can you resent your one shot at heaven, even if it makes you feel like a fool?

So here I am, sitting on a comically tiny stool at a community college, surrounded by overgrown children, just waiting to lay eyes on my Sweet with a silly smile on my face. And it is all worth it the moment she walks in. She's stunning, that magic immediately filling the air between us with electricity. As soon as she places her stuff down, her eyes fly to my station, checking for me.

I don't look away. I'm not ashamed to be caught staring at her. The closer we get to Halloween, the bolder I can be. She is going to be mine, one way or another, so what's the point of being bashful? But when our eyes meet, she looks ...disconcerted. She's biting her lip in *nervousness* instead of arousal. Quickly, she looks away and goes to organize the lab manuals for today's class. She keeps repeatedly pushing her hair back, just for it to fall into her face again. She's so *flustered*. She wasn't even this phased when I chased her with a knife. *What the fuck is happening?*

It took everything in me not to drag her out into the hallway and make her tell me what was wrong so I could immediately solve whatever is distressing her like this. I think the poor kid, who ended up my lab partner this semester, was more scared than normal of my demeanor. The *need* to fix whatever is causing her distress has my pulse so loud in my ears that I can barely hear his timid requests for me to pass a certain supply or measure something out.

It only got worse when she slipped over to our station just long enough to say, "Damian, could you please come see me before you leave today? Thanks," and practically ran away before I could respond.

My brain flooded with panic that I had to bury before it escaped. *Did she figure it out? Does she know it's you? HOW? What did you fuck up! ...No. Breathe. If she knew it was you, then she would've shown up to class with the cops, not asked to talk.* But that didn't make me feel any better. Suddenly, I was analyzing every detail of Saturday night. *Did I misread it? Does she feel differently about how it went? Has having more time to think about what she saw scared her? Does she not want to see me again?* My eyes fall to my scabbed knuckles and I hide my hands under the desk, hoping she didn't notice they look rougher than they had Saturday night.

The thought that she was upset about something from Saturday was actually more nervewracking than the idea that she had figured out I was her stalker. We can work through that. It'd be awkward, sure, but if she's enjoyed her time with me as myself *and* as her masked tormentor, then it shouldn't be too hard to sell the combo. That's basically the plan anyway, just a little faster than I hoped if she figured it out. But her *not* liking me? That's going to make things a lot more difficult on us both.

I'm not giving her up. There's no way. I can't. I already know she enjoys our masked little games, so if she decides she doesn't like me as a man then fine. All she'll ever get is the masked monster from me, including when I take her somewhere far away and remote to keep her all to myself if I have to.

Somewhere in the middle of brainstorming about exactly how I'd kidnap Celeste and where we'd go, my lab partner wraps up our experiment. I notice him packing up and offer to do the clean up since I know he did more than his share of the work today. He didn't need me to offer twice and scurried away as soon as his bag zipped. I took my time cleaning, attempting to prepare myself for what might be coming. But I'm not sure if even my self control can handle something like this.

When I'm done sanitizing the station...for the *second* time, I finally make my way over to Celeste.

"Ms. Carroll? You wanted to see me? If I didn't turn something in, I swear my dog ate it."

She laughs, but there's still a nervous tinge to it. She tucks her hair back again and isn't making eye contact with me, "No, no, Damian it isn't about your work. At least not like that...Look, about Saturday night..."

My stomach is twisted into such tight knots it feels like my organs must be ripping away from one another. *This can't be fucking happening.*

"I don't know how you feel about it, but I went and asked Professor Beck to take over grading your work before class today."

What? The confusion must have been apparent on my face, because she finally looks up when I don't answer her and her face flashes a deep crimson as she continues, "Because I can no longer impartially evaluate your work, Damian. Look," she breathes deep like she's preparing to do something difficult, "I haven't been able to stop thinking about Saturday. I had a great time, and I really like you. I don't know if it felt like a date to you, or if you even *like* me like that, but if you do, would you want to come to my party this Friday? I throw this movie under the stars party every year -"

The sudden mix of relief and ecstasy that washes over me has to be what narcotics feel like. *She's asking me to be her date. She was just as nervous at the thought that I didn't like her as I was when I thought she might not like me. Though I wonder if she would've kidnapped me anyway like I would've her?*

My smile is so large I can feel it straining the muscles of my face and I couldn't give a damn. "I'd love to be your date."

Her eyes light up in that way I adore. She's biting her lip again, but in excitement instead of nervousness, exactly as it should be. She excitedly gives me the details before I leave her to finish up the lab with the remaining students. I am practically floating out of the building to my car. Instinctively, I want to lecture myself for being ridiculous, but I'm too happy for the negativity to even manifest itself. *This woman really is something otherworldly. Nothing else explains this kind of effect.*

But just as quickly as she flooded me with joy, the sight of the tall slender man leaning against my hood, smoking, drains me of it all. *Damn it.*

I start towards my door, intending to get in and not even acknowledge him, when I catch sight of his two lackeys from last time coming in from each end of the car row. *I wonder if she'd still want me to come to her party if I can make bail for running three people over before Friday?*

Kage's voice grates my nerves. "Don't worry, cuz, they're just trying to keep me safe. My guys are pretty loyal and apparently they don't believe me when I tell them you wouldn't hurt me."

"Money doesn't buy real loyalty."

He nods, shaking the cigarette in his hand towards me, "True. If it could, then I wouldn't be back here looking for someone I can actually trust, Damian."

I open the truck door so it sits between us, popping a caramel into my mouth, hoping yet again that the taste of her will calm me. "I already told you, Kage, I'm done with that life, and I'm done with you."

He finally turns to face me, a poor attempt at mock offense plastered on his face. "Done? With family?" His cruel laugh cuts through the air. "That's not how this works, Damian. You're a LaCroix. I let you have your fucking sabbatical to play 'normal', but it's time to come home. You need to sort your shit out here and come to terms with that. *Soon*. My patience is running thin."

I look at him in disgust over the car door and spit at his feet. "Fuck off, Kage. If you really needed someone you could trust, you wouldn't want anyone you had to strong-arm into it. I don't know why you've suddenly got a bug up your ass about me, but I suggest you move on. We both know you've never liked having to sleep with one eye open."

He stares into my eyes, those icy blues, that look just like my mother's and every other fucked up LaCroix's but mine, are laced with a threat. "Maybe I just miss my family. Not many of us left. Speaking of which, that pretty little lab teacher of yours looks an awful lot like the witch on your arm, is she a LaCroix to be? Maybe I should teach her what it means to be one of us."

My vision flashes red as the rage injects itself into my bloodstream like an adrenaline shot. I lunge forward viciously, slamming into my door, and damaging the hinges. Kage has a glock out and pointed right at me in a flash as my fists are turning white, gripping the edge of the window.

"Bring her with you if she can keep her mouth shut, or bang her and get it out of your system. I don't give a damn, cuz. But get your affairs in this little shithole of a town handled, because playtime is over."

He keeps the gun trained on me until he's in the car with his men and leaving. I slam the door closed so hard I'm surprised I don't knock it the rest of the way off the hinges. *FUCK!* My mother's shrill tirades come to mind. *Retribution will always come to the guilty. You are an evil boy and your sins will haunt you. Sick trees only bare rotten fruit, no matter what you do, God knows what you are and he will punish you.*

I barely make it back into the car before the need to pummel something takes over. I beat the shit out of my steering wheel until the exhaustion finally makes me stop to breathe. *Fine, Mother. The LaCroix tree is sick, and if Kage forces my hand, I swear I'll cut it down before I let it poison Celeste. Huh, who would've ever thought I would end up the Lord's retribution?*

Celeste

"Savannah, can you light the citronella lanterns? I want to run off the mosquitoes as soon as possible!"

"What? You want to be the only thing biting on your hunky electrician tonight? GREEDY!"

I filled the girls in on what's been developing between Damian and I over the last two weeks. Needless to say, the teasing has been incessant ever since but at least they're more excited for me now. When I first told them, they both looked nervous and brought up my stalker. Not that I blame them, it's the exact same thought I had before.

But I didn't really want to tell them about the barfight that changed my mind because I wasn't sure if they'd judge Damian too easily...or me for basically risking him because I think he's capable of defending us. So instead I lied, which I feel bad about, but no one's perfect. *I hope his knuckles have healed up more since Tuesday. They looked rough, honestly rougher than I would've expected, and I know Savannah's ass will just ask. She has absolutely no filter.*

I told the girls that I hadn't heard from the stalker since the "see you soon" note. That he'd skipped out on the gift with the last quarter moon. I even pitched that maybe he saw me out with Damian and got spooked, or that he got bored when I didn't freak out like he clearly wanted when he left the note. They both seemed hesitant to buy that, but it didn't take much of listening to me gush over Damian for them to jump on the pro-new-relationship bandwagon, stalker be damned.

They both came over early today to help me set up for tonight. This is the biggest event I throw every year. We still have to string up the fairy lights on posts to make a perimeter for the backyard, but we already have all the lawn chairs, throw blankets, torches, and the firepit set up. I purchased enough wood to maintain an impressive blaze for the majority of the night, carefully contained in a pit of sand and cheap paving stones. I put a tall, standing campfire grate over the pit so we can make old school stovetop popcorn and roast spiced apple halves over it. I also have sticks laid off to the side for marshmallows. Savannah and April just finished hanging the giant white sheet over the back of my house, pulling it tight to create a makeshift projector screen, while I've been working on the concessions table.

There's a massive spread of movie box candies, s'mores ingredients, mini foil popcorn tins, veggie trays, and closer to the event I'll bring out the halved and sliced apples with caramel dips I have prepped in the fridge. I also have a giant cooler of ice and a variety of sodas, lemonades, and a crockpot on an extension cord just so I can have spiked hot apple cider. A bonfire is fun for the atmosphere and treats, but there is nothing better at keeping you warm on a fall night than hot apple cider with Fireball whiskey.

"I'm excited to meet him, Cee," April chimes in chipperly. She might be more delighted about Damian and me than I am. I don't know why, honestly. After Issac, I expected her to be a little more wary of the men I bring around, but she has been gung-ho about him all week.

"I just hope tonight isn't too much. I mean, we've kinda been out once and now I'm bringing him to an event where he has to meet all my closest friends and whoever they invited out as well? I didn't really think this through beyond," I turn to the girls and shake my fingers in the air like I'm casting magic, "romantic bonfire and horror movie cuddles."

Savannah laughs at me, "If your living room decor didn't scare him off then I doubt a dozen strangers will."

God, I hope not. When I started this tradition back in college, I wanted to share it with as many other people as possible, but I'm not particularly social the rest of the year, so I didn't have a big guestlist. My solution was to let my closest friends invite whoever they wanted and then have them give me a headcount so I could be prepared. I've done it the same ever since.

I was so nervous to invite him to this, but I had to do *something*. I certainly could've thought more about what I should ask him to but this was the first event I had coming up and I hadn't been able to stop thinking about him since the diner. That kiss that *didn't* happen has been haunting me. I was a mess trying to figure out if I was more into him than he was me, and I probably never would've had the guts to ask him out if he hadn't slipped up at the end of our goodbye. He didn't kiss me, but he called me *Celeste* instead of *Ms. Carroll*. It may seem stupid, but it felt like it meant something. And now he's coming here tonight as my date, *so apparently it did*.

I check my watch. We have about an hour until sundown, and then everyone should start arriving. The marathon will begin at eight once it's solidly dark, and go well into the early hours of the morning like it does every year. I glance over at the chairs and picture Damian and I huddled together, me on his lap, both of us wrapped up in a blanket while we watch the movie and I immediately get butterflies.

But they quickly shrivel up and die when the image of a pumpkin face, peering through the stalks, invades my mind. At this point I'm pretty confident, *granted perhaps stupidly*, that my stalker won't actually hurt me in our games. But would that persist if he saw me with someone else?

Damn, maybe I need to go ahead and start on that cider and Fireball mix.

Damian

When I pull into her driveway, I'm surprised by the number of cars there. I know she said "party", but I don't think I've ever seen the majority of these vehicles, and I've watched her interactions pretty damn closely over the last year. *Fucking crowds. Great.*

I grab the small bouquet of black roses from the passenger seat before sliding out of the truck. I pull at the ends of my sleeves and adjust my shirt. I haven't cared about what I was going to wear to an event in so long, I forgot how fucking arduous it can be to decide. I spent an hour doing loops through my rather small wardrobe, trying to find something that felt nice enough for a party host's date but casual enough to be outside and to meet her friends. Granted, I already know a lot about Savannah, April, and Eric, but they don't know me. Trying to come off "normal" is hard enough when you look the part, I certainly don't need anymore obstacles.

Finally, I settled on a red and black flannel long-sleeve shirt, dark jeans, and black boots. Three visible pieces of clothing and it took me a fucking hour to decide. *What the hell is happening to me?* The last time I put effort like this into picking outfits was when I was deciding what clothes I didn't want to risk ruining with blood.

I take a deep breath and slide on my mask. Not the pumpkin one that my Sweet has become so fond of, but the "typical guy" one I wear when I have to be around others. The kinds of people who can't handle the severity and violence of the world. The ones who have never experienced true horrors. The ones who would run screaming from a peek into the darkness of my past. The ones who aren't like my Celeste.

I follow her elaborate display of glowing jack-o'-lanterns that have been placed along one side of the wrap-around porch to guide the guests to the rear of the house. As soon as I round the corner to her backyard, I'm impressed with what the ladies put together. I was slammed at work today, so I didn't get to spy as much as I would've liked, but Celeste's yard has been transformed into a cozy camp social spot. There's just under a dozen people milling about in the warm glow cast by the strings of lights and the torches that trim the space. A collection of chairs are scattered all around, with people mingling as they snack and break into smaller groups. *Not as bad as it could be for a "party".* I recognize a few people.

A large pile of firewood is being coaxed into a blaze by a lanky guy with big, round glasses, Eric. April is standing behind him laughing and sipping on a drink when she catches sight of me and her eyes bug out. She glances down to the roses, cracks a smile, and dashes off around the house.

Savannah is standing by a table full of snacks talking to a small group of people. She's far more subtle, but I catch her sizing me up from the side of her gaze while she doesn't even break the stride of her conversation.

Interesting...They both picked me out on sight. She's been talking about me. In detail, clearly.

April comes rushing back from around the porch practically dragging Celeste with her, but she tries to slow to a normal stride as they come into view, causing my Sweet to stumble and almost drop a tray of apple slices and cups of...caramel? *Really?* Sometimes I wonder if she actually is a witch and this whole time she's been puppetting me in some kind of master game of cat and mouse. I think I'm stalking her and making all these plans meanwhile she's actually just letting me play pretend and been setting her own hooks from the start.

She's in a pair of jeans and boots with a fishnet tank top on and a tied off red button down over it. The top is unbuttoned completely, but knotted under the bust to cover and cup her ample breasts just right, the bottom edge of the fabric cinching around her waist to accentuate her curvaceous figure. Her jeans fit her like they are painted on. She's sporting her signature black lipstick and looking like she could be the star of a hard rock music video. But when my eyes finally meet Celeste's, she lights up brighter than all the jack-o'-lanterns along her porch, and suddenly the smile on my face isn't as forced as it was mere seconds ago. I stride over to her before I'm even aware I'm moving, just like I did on that porch last year.

"Here, why don't you trade me?" I hold out the bouquet with one hand, while I take the apple tray from her with the other.

She blushes, "Oh, Damian, they're beautiful. Thank you." Flustered, she continues, "Damian, this is April, April, Damian."

April looks like a balloon that might pop, she's bursting at the seams with energy, practically bouncing in place. "Hi! It's so great to meet you! Cee, you go get those in some water and I'll take him over to the snack table to set these down and get situated. Grab the movies as well and whatever else you might need, okay? Okay! See you in a minute!"

Next thing I know, this small, bouncy brunette has me by the free arm and is dragging me away in the same manner she had been Celeste just a minute ago...or at least trying to. We didn't move an inch until I started to go with her. As soon as my Sweet was out of sight, Savannah was excusing herself from her group and making a beeline to meet April and me at the other end of the concessions.

Boldly, Savannah greets me with, "So, we've heard a lot about you." Arms crossed, leaned onto her back leg, and her eyebrow cocked, it's clear she has her reservations about me.

"All good things!" April interjects, clearly perturbed by Savannah's tone. "Look, we don't have long before Cee will be back and we just wanted to say a few things to you, privately."

It's my turn to shift an eyebrow, "Well, please then, carry on, ladies. What's on your minds?"

April jumps in before Savannah can, "Cee has had some real shitty luck with guys before. Like, *really* shitty. We are both sure you're great," Savannah huffs beside her and April shoots her a look, "but *if* you aren't actually, just please don't hurt her, okay? She hasn't stepped back into the dating pool in a *long* time, and neither of us want to see her get burned right out of the gate."

Savannah looks at me with an icyness that makes the hairs on the back of even my neck rise. *Interesting.* "April's being nice. If you hurt her, I will fucking kill you."

Ha. Unlikely. But something about the look in her eyes makes me believe she might actually try. *Hm, perhaps I'll end up liking Celeste's friends more than I assumed...as long as they don't get in the way.*

I look at them both intensely, trying to convey my seriousness without coming off too crazy, "I can promise you both, I would never do anything to hurt Celeste. I wouldn't say I'm great per se, but I'm smart enough to know that she is special and I'm lucky to spend time with her."

April appears satisfied, glowing at my response, but Savannah is still watching me with a cynical gaze. That is until suddenly her face switches to an expression just as friendly as April's as she says, "It's so nice to meet you, Damian, I'm Savannah, I work with Cee at the bar," offering me her hand.

I shake it, catching on just a moment before her perfume announces Celeste's return. Her hand touches my back, her nails trailing just an inch down the center of it as she comes up beside me. It takes every bit of self control I have not to shiver in front of everyone. *Fuck.*

"So what are you guys talking about without me?"

I answer quickly, hoping to cover for the girls and earn their trust. "I was just saying the corn stalks out here are very atmospheric but I'm surprised they hadn't been harvested yet."

April shakes her head enthusiastically, "Yeah! And I was about to tell him how most of the farms out here don't grow sweet corn. It's a lot of yellow dent corn that's used in feed, fuels, and other products. It has to dry out completely before it's usable. Sweet corn is harvested early because they want it juicy, but it's cheaper for farmers to let the dent corn dry on the stalk rather than to harvest it and have to send it to an industrial dryer. It's normal to see corn fields out here till late October and November or even sometimes December, depending on how wet of a year it's been."

Savannah looks at me inquisitively, "How long have you lived in this area? Haven't you ever noticed that?"

"I guess I just didn't pay that much attention. I've lived in Ammerton for a while, but honestly I don't get out of the town limits often."

"Be nice, Savannah!" Celeste laughs, patting me on the back and looking up at me with humor and reassurance in her eyes and I feel like I could get lost in those brilliant emeralds. *Is she worried I'm nervous or that her friends might run me off? This woman has no idea. It would take an army to keep me away from her.*

April rolls her eyes, "Is Savannah *ever* that nice? Now let's get snacks, drinks, and the movies going! It looks like Eric's got the fire steady and I'm dying for a s'more!"

The guests collect their concessions and move the chairs into little clusters across the yard. Celeste makes us a plate overflowing with treats to share, tosses a popcorn tin on the fire, and insists I at least try one cup of the spiked apple cider as Eric and I make a grouping of five chairs off to the side with a good view of the screen.

The girls all settle in, Savannah in the middle with April and Celeste on either side, allowing Eric and I to sit next to our dates. Celeste scoots closer to me, so that the arms of our chairs touch, creating an impromptu table to lay our snacks on. Immediately, the apples and caramel catch my eye and I want to feed them to her, just so I can kiss her right after to savor the flavor directly from her lips.

"So what movies are we doing tonight?" Eric asks.

Celeste smiles, standing to go load the first one into the DVD player connected to the projector. "*Scream, Scream 2,* and *Scream 4.*"

Eric looked shocked, "Wait, why not *Scream 3*? Is there a horror movie you don't actually own?"

April and Savannah both sigh before they chime in, speaking in unison with Celeste, "The only thing scary about *Scream 3* is Gale Weather's bangs." *I guess she's expressed that opinion a few times.*

Celeste whirls around on her heels, sticking her tongue out at her mocking echoes, before spinning back around to her task at hand, showing off that perfect round ass. *Damn, she's adorable and a fucking wet dream. I don't know how she does both.*

"*Scream*'s a great classic, but I can't believe they have Drew Barrymore missing the question about who is the killer in the first Friday the 13th when she's supposed to be a scary movie fan, that's so basic." But as soon as I finish my sentence, the looks on the faces around me make me wonder if I've made a mistake.

Celeste doesn't react, just continuing to skip the trailers to get to the DVD selection screen faster. I down the entire cup of apple cider in one go. *Damn, that is really good. And really dangerous, I didn't taste a bit of the alcohol.*

Eric snatches the glass from me, "Let me refill that for you, you're going to need it."

April whispers, "Go ahead and grab him an extra glass too, might as well save someone the trip."

Oh shit, what the fuck did I do?

Once the movie starts, Celeste skips back over to us, collecting our popcorn from the bonfire on the way, with an overly sweet smile on her face as she sits down next to me. I've never been so on edge around her, even when she came at me with a knife.

She leans in close to my face, batting her eyelashes as she grabs a handful of popcorn and tosses it in her mouth, "Now what was that nonsense I overheard you say while I was setting up the movie?" The mouthful of crunchy popcorn muffling her words. Eric returns, handing me two glasses, and takes his seat with a look of pity on his face.

I feel like I've made a mistake. "Um, well I just said I thought they made Drew Barrymore miss a silly question."

She enthusiastically nods her head in agreement. "Mhm, mhm. *Casey,* who was under extreme stress in a wild, dangerous, and sudden situation, did make a common horror trivia mistake, which is probably why Ghostface resorted to that question after she got other ones correct. Do you think you can do better? I won't even put your life on the line, just your pride." She winks, her eyes alight with mischief.

Oh yeah, I've definitely made a mistake. Instinctually, I'm leaning back from her intense stare, "Well, I...uh...have a feeling I haven't seen nearly as many movies as you have, so that's probably a waste of time."

She throws her head back laughing, making the other little groups jump, the glee cutting through the tension of the infamous "what's your favorite scary movie?" phone call.

"Oh nonsense, you said *Scream* is a great classic, right? So you've clearly watched it before? I'll only ask you questions about it!"

I look around the group for back up. Eric is watching the movie, Savannah is looking at me smugly, and April is staring at Celeste with concern on her face. My Sweet is sipping on her cider while April is leaning into Savannah and asking how many she's had.

Celeste looks at me so innocently, but I don't trust it. That bratty streak is alive and well in those pretty green eyes. "Oh, come on, Damian, just three questions about the first *Scream* movie. You can do that, I'm sure," her smile grows wicked, "but if you can't then..." She drags on the pause dramatically, "I get to give you a dare you can't refuse!"

What the fuck, she really did take us all to summer camp. "Okay, fine. You're on."

She giggles and my heart skips a beat. I watch the wheels turning in her head as I take another sip of the cider. *I wonder how strong this is, I really can't taste it at all, but it's clearly helping her unwind.*

"Okay, okay, we will start easy - who is the killer in *Scream*?"

I smirk at her, "There are two, Billy Loomis and Stu Macher."

She throws one hand up in the air enthusiastically, "Correct!" Immediately, she pulls it back, jerking it over her mouth, muffling her giggle at her own outburst. *Damn, she's cute.* "Okay, question number two," now she's whispering. "What movie is the group watching at Stu's house party that leads to Randy's infamous lecture about the "rules" of a horror movie?"

Oh shit. My eyes flash around the group and they are all watching us curiously, but it's clear I'm on my own in this challenge. Apparently, I must've poked the bear by taking a jab at this movie. *There is a giant Scream movie poster in the living room. Probably should've considered that, dumbass.*

She's staring at me expectantly, "Hmm?"

"Umm, well uhh, it's a classic film..."

Her smile looks down right twisted and menacing in the firelight. *Hot.* "Oh, Damian, I need more than *that*."

Fuck, she is so distracting. She looks like she could eat me alive right now...and I want to let her. "Uh, some dude asks when they are going to see Jamie Lee's tits, right? So I'm going to say *Halloween*."

She sits up and back in her chair, crossing her legs. Her alluringly painted black lips pursed in a mix of amusement and annoyance. "Jamie Lee Curtis is one of the most iconic scream queens of all time, she's starred in a lot of horror movies, but you guessed the right one. Lucky you."

I feel like a damn teenager. I don't know how a fucking little trivia game can feel like foreplay, but the way she's coming for me, trying to trip me up so she can force me to do something, all while she looks that good lit by dancing firelight, has me squirming in my seat from more than just the intensity of her gaze.

She bites her bottom lip, letting her teeth slowly rake over it as it slips out, just like she did when she kissed me last year, before a smug, victorious grin sets in. "What movie is Billy quoting when he reveals himself as a killer by saying, 'We all go a little mad sometimes'?"

I jump in immediately, "Ha! It's *Alice in Wonderland*! I win!" I sit back confidently, lifting my cup for another drink. But I stall when I see the sympathetic looks on April's and Eric's faces and Savannah's satisfied smirk.

Slightly afraid to, I slowly turn back towards Celeste, finding her face extremely close to mine, an almost bloodthirsty look on it. The viciousness is perfectly highlighted by Drew Barrymore's, sorry, *Casey's*, screams in the background as she's being gutted on the screen. "Nuh-uh. He's quoting *Psycho*. Norman Bates. You lose, handsome."

I can't help but smile at her complimenting me, even if I feel like I'm in trouble. I've gone into situations, knowing damn well it's a fight to the death and I may not make it out, and I still didn't feel as nervous as I do right now under her malicious gaze. *Why the fuck am I hard?*

"So what's it gonna be, Cee?" April asks.

"Yeah, as fun as it is to watch y'all's foreplay, I do want to get to the movie eventually, so just put the man out of his misery and give him his punishment, oh great queen of horror," Savannah adds playfully.

Celeste's eyes rake down over my body, making my cock twitch in my jeans. "I dare you...to be my chair for the rest of the night."

Well shit...I should've missed them all.

Celeste

April's shocked little gasp at my dare makes me giggle. I've probably had one too many of my spiked apple ciders if I can be this bold, but I haven't been able to get that image out of my head since the party set-up. I want to sit in his lap, wrapped up in a blanket by the fire, and watch the movies.

Who cares about a missed opportunity in a parking lot, when this could be the setting for our first kiss? It's perfect.

Though I should probably stop drinking before I end up trying to ride him under the blanket, convinced I'm being subtle enough no one would know when in reality everyone would probably be scarred for life.

I'm staring into his molten reddish hazel eyes, desperate for him to pull me onto his lap. My pussy is pulsing with desire as his sinful smirk spreads across his face. "Well, I don't really get to say no, do I?" But his lustful look makes it very clear that he has absolutely no desire to argue.

"No, you don't," I reply very decidedly as I pick up our snacks and wait expectantly in front of him, not bothering to hide the smugness on my face.

He holds his arms out in a welcoming gesture as he leans back in the chair and spreads his legs to make room. *A sexy throne just for me.* I should probably be concerned about a cheap lawn chair holding us both when he barely fits in it himself but I couldn't give a damn right now.

I sit down slowly on one of his legs, teasing each of us with a little wiggle as I get comfy. His hands twitch on the armrests. *Good.* I throw both of my legs over his other one and lay the snacks on my thighs. I catch Savannah rolling her eyes, trying to hide a smile before she turns her focus back to the screen. April and Eric are cuddled up together under a blanket, whispering back and forth. Everyone else's attention is wrapped up in snacks or the movie. The crickets are playing a subtle symphony in the background as the fairy lights sway in the breeze and the fire crackles. The things that always make this one of the best nights of the year are all here...

And now I have him as well. I look back at Damian to find him staring at me shamelessly with flames dancing in his eyes. I know they're just reflections but *God* they look like they are living and breathing inside his pupils, raging only for me. An inferno that could engulf me...and I will happily burn.

We barely know each other, yet he's entranced by me in this moment. *Even I can see it.* The way he's watching me like I'm a dream that might dissipate with the next breeze, a slightly desperate need and tender fear in the tremble of his lips as his eyes dip to mine. *I don't know why he'd want me like this so soon...but I feel it too. This heat coiling in my stomach...and it is far more than the familiar warmth of the cider and the whiskey.* I watch the subtle bounce of his throat as he swallows, breaking our stare to quickly reach for a slice of apple which he swipes through the caramel.

No. We aren't running from this.

I don't know who is in the fields or if I'm being watched. I don't know what this night is going to cost me with my stalker so it better be fucking worth *it.*

He tosses the apple in his mouth, a dollop of the caramel falling off onto his bottom lip. He goes to wipe it away with his thumb as he chews rapidly and I don't know where the hell it comes from but what happens next stuns us both.

I grab his wrist, stopping his hand as I run my other one through his hair, tilting his head back towards me. My eyes flash up to his before they cut back to his mouth. I lean in suddenly, licking the drop of caramel from the swell of his lip. I freeze, savoring the sweetness on my tongue, looking at him through my eyelashes but refusing to retreat. Our lips are so close we can feel the heat of each other's breath on our tender skin.

His eyes are shocked...and trying to contain a war. I can see it. I don't know if he's fighting some internalized lesson from society about appropriateness, audiences, or time and place, *but I don't care.* This is *our* moment. *Do it Damian.*

Suddenly his arms wrap around me, one pulling me closer, the other running up the curve of my back, molding against my body. His fingers brush along the nape of my neck, giving me chills, before his hand takes hold of it. He pulls me in, crushing our lips together. The moment they meet, we both devolve like two people who have been wandering a desert that just found an oasis in one another.

He tastes like a potion of all my favorite indulgences. The sweet tartness of apples and caramel, the burn of cinnamon whiskey, and the saliva of a man who's hungry for me. I melt into him. Our lips move with a tender reverence, as if we are sharing a holy rite, while they tremble with this need we share.

I bite tenderly into his bottom lip as he starts to break away for a breath. *Fuck air, you aren't going anywhere.* Sucking gently to pull him back into me. My nails dig into his flesh, marking him. I don't want to let him go. *I can't.* I don't know what's gotten into me, but it feels like I'm finally surrendering to a secret craving I didn't even know I had.

His tongue probes against the junction of our lips and I open, inviting him in. They tangle passionately as we kiss deeper with a fervor that leaves us a mess of gasps and moans, chests heaving as we try to catch our breath when we finally break it. My eyes are hooded, heavy with the heady arousal that is racing through my entire body. But once I finally manage to open them completely, I am met by a delectably sinful smirk smeared in black lipstick and reddish hazel eyes that are alight with just as much delirium as I am feeling.

Oh yeah...that was definitely worth whatever comes. Screw it. Do your worst, Pumpkin Face, I'd fucking do it again.

Damian

I think Scream *is my favorite horror franchise now.* I've been in heaven for hours...or at least with her, if not 'in' her yet. Celeste and I have been bundled up under a blanket as we've watched the movies, sneaking kisses and laughing with her friends. She's glowing, happy, and carefree. It's infectious.

I don't ever remember feeling this truly...relaxed and satisfied. Not the type of satisfaction that comes from a hot meal or sexual release, but the one that settles into your soul. The one that heals the emptiness inside someone. I don't care who else is here or what we're doing, I don't care who I was or who I am now, *as long as* she can glow like that while being in my arms, then the world is right. Everything else will work itself out.

The party started to wind down while the last movie was playing. Between the copious amount of food and warm alcohol Celeste provided her guests, sleepiness started to overtake people. Most everyone has cleared out other than her personal friends and us. *I'm not moving from this spot until she fucking makes me. We can stay out here all night watching movies just the two of us as far as I'm concerned.*

We're all decently buzzed and well past caring how loud we are with our commentary on the movie. April chimes in, "That dude's whole motive being 'well, Kirby didn't pay attention to me, so I started killing for this other girl that put out but wouldn't be caught dead with me in public' is so *lame*. Like, as if. Dude can't really be that hard up."

Savannah shrugs, "I mean, who knows? Maybe some women just drive people crazy? I could see it."

April squeals, "Bull. You don't see women you are willing to go on more than three or four dates with from fear that they might think y'all are *actually* dating. Don't pretend you think anyone is worth being 'crazy' about."

I don't know if anybody else picks up on it, but a cloud of irritation passes over Savannah's face before she quickly packs it away, leaning back in her chair to sip on her drink more.

"Fumbling Kirby would be kinda like fumbling Celeste, and I don't think anyone would handle that well," I add, gently rubbing my hand up and down the dip of her lower back.

She blushes, either from the compliment or the alcohol, as she laughs, "Well, Issac managed just fine, but I appreciate the sentiment."

"If that's so, then why did he call me last week asking about you?" Eric manages to say right before April's backhand connects with his stomach, trying to shut him up.

"Eric!" She hisses.

"Oh shit, sorry, it slipped out."

Who's this Issac? It wouldn't be obvious to anyone watching her, but I can feel the tension in Celeste's body that has suddenly turned her into a statue on top of my knee.

"What do you mean that *Issac* called you asking about *me?*" she grits through her teeth. But she doesn't sound angry, more like she can barely move her jaw with how tightly wound her entire body is right now.

Eric stumbles over his words, "I didn't tell him anything Cee. I said I hadn't heard from you and he knows better than to -"

"We were going to tell you tomorrow," April interrupts, "I just know how much this party means to you and I didn't want to upset you before you could enjoy it."

"*We?*" Celeste is suddenly standing, gone from my grasp. Her light and warmth are rapidly melting away. I can feel the cold emptiness in my soul starting to creep back in. *I could kill these fucking people right now for dimming my Sweet's happiness.* "Savannah, did you know about this too?"

Savannah stares into her drink, unwilling to meet Celeste's eyes. "I was against not telling you, but I was outvoted."

"Oh! That's great, so my life is a fucking democracy where I don't even get a vote now? Really, guys?" She grabs up her drink and downs it. "I love you all but I can't do this. Enjoy the rest of the movie, see yourselves out, and call me tomorrow ...actually let's make it Sunday. Give me a fucking day." She spins on her heels and starts to storm off.

How much does she really care about these people? Because I want to coat myself in their blood right now. *Them and whoever the fuck this Issac is.*

She whips back around, "Damian! Oh fuck, I'm so sorry, um, if you want to finish the movie, just knock on my front door before you leave so I can tell you bye, okay?"

I'm up and out of my seat in a second, "I'd rather go with you, if you'll have me."

She looks down at the ground, pushing her hair back behind her ear as she considers it. Without a sound, she nods her head and I'm instantly by her side, wrapping her up in a blanket and walking her away from the *menaces*.

I whisper as we shuffle along the side of the house, passing all the jack-o'-lanterns with their dwindling candles, "Are you okay?" *Stupid fucking question.*

Breathing deep, she sighs as she answers me, "Yeah, I'm sorry...I was just having a great time and I wasn't...Well, I wasn't expecting news like that. It kinda hit me like a truck." She pulls the blanket tighter around herself, as if a chill is settling inside of her. It only makes the one inside of me grow icier. *Who is this motherfucker?*

I place an arm over her shoulders as we walk around the corner of the porch in silence. Celeste doesn't pull away, but she doesn't lean into me either. She's stiff, lost in her own mind, and closed off, even while she's trying to be kind to me. So different from what we were just minutes ago. *This guy really did a number on her.*

We sit down together on the front steps and look out over the sea of corn stalks, waving in the wind like an ocean with gentle swells passing by. A beautiful full moon is up in the sky, illuminating everything in an elegant, pale glow. It's so clear on this side of the house without all the intrusions from the light pollution.

I never used to pay any attention to the moon. I couldn't have given a shit about what phase it was in or how things looked in its light a year ago. But after seeing her standing in it that first time and then spending so many nights sitting outside her house bathed by it, I developed a real appreciation for the moon. She introduced poetry to my life without even speaking it. Celeste has changed me in so many subtle ways, I don't think even I could identify all of them.

"Issac is my ex, as I'm sure you gathered," she offers, breaking our silence.

I turn to look at her as she continues to watch the stalks sway. But I don't speak, not wanting to risk an intrusion pulling her from wherever she is mentally that she's willing to share this with me.

"I left him four years ago, but we were together for almost six before that. He was my first, well *only,* major relationship." She brushes her hair back behind her ear as she scoffs. "Fucking twenty-nine and I've had one long-term relationship. Damn. I don't know why I just told you that, I'm sure that looks great."

I'm confused and too curious not to ask so I reply gently, "Why wouldn't it?"

"Because it implies something is wrong with me," she says softly into the night, "No one before Issac worked out for long, either because I was unlikable or too picky, then I was too broken to be appealing or to trust anyone after. Somehow in thirteen years of dating, I've only been in a relationship with one person, a shitty person on top of it. That isn't exactly a great resume to give the hot guy I just spent half the night kissing." She drops her head in her hands, elbows propped on her knees.

I stare at her in disbelief. She has managed to make herself believe that other people not seeing her value and unrivaled divinity or treating her with respect is her *own* fault? How can she think that shows anything but those people's idiocy and unworthiness? She deserves someone who worships every part of her, darkness included. *I'm so devoted, I'd be willing to make blood sacrifices to appease that darkness if she demanded it.*

"Celeste...that's not what that implies."

"Yeah? What does it then?" She still hasn't lifted her head to look at me, but I can't tear my eyes away from her.

"That you are a woman who didn't waste time on relationships she knew weren't what she wanted and then was loyal and devoted, perhaps to a fault, when she found someone she thought was her person. But you've never been properly seen or loved for who you are, so when you finally picked yourself, *as you should*, over someone who didn't deserve you, you needed a while to heal. You didn't want to hurt yourself or others in the process, so you took time instead of risks. I see maturity, wisdom, and a good heart."

She half laughs under her hands. "What the *fuck*. Where did you come up with that? What kind of play is that?" Sitting up suddenly, she starts tossing her hands around with as much frantic energy as the words are tumbling from her mouth, "Look, I'm sorry. Maybe this was a bad idea. I'm sure you aren't trying to *play* me, but that's just...*so different* from anything I've ever been told."

Damn, there's the trust issues. "Well I don't know who said bullshit like that, but it's not true, Celeste."

"Practically everyone throughout my life. I mean, maybe not in so many words, but I have always had to be the 'good', 'right', or 'proper' one, or else the outrage or scandal that ensued was my fault. My existence was defined by the reactions I caused in people, why do you think I limit who I share it with so much now, Damian?"

The cider and whiskey is making her very open and honest tonight. She continues, "First my parents wanted their typical, all-American, sweet, quiet, girl-next-door daughter to fit the white picket fence image. I got good grades, I stayed out of trouble, but that rock music or colored streak in my hair was not acceptable," she changes her voice, imitating a man's, "not respectable."

She turns to me, her eyes searching mine. Those emeralds shining in the moonlight as the tears she's fighting back well up. "Then I went off to school - all the way across the country. Freedom and the ability to be myself within my grasp. But I met Issac my first semester and I just let him take as much control of me as I had resented my parents for because I *thought* he loved me."

The first tear overflows, leaving a path of moisture shimmering on her cheek and my gut wrenches. These aren't the same as the tears that she has shed in her bed under my touch. These aren't cathartic acceptance, they come from a raw wound she still hasn't healed completely. Her suffering, *real suffering*, kills me.

She stares out into the night again. "The woman you see today is who I've always wanted to be. Yet somehow, I believed that someone could *actually* love me while they simultaneously forced me into a mold of what they wanted. Issac never cared about me, he just enjoyed that I was clay he could shape into his dream girl because I thought that's what love was. I let myself believe that all his little critiques, and rules, and judgements were genuinely for concern about me and my success. But the longer we were together, the more obvious it became. Nothing I wanted or dreamed of mattered unless it was also already important to him. Every choice I made had to be approved or else he would harass me about my 'immaturity' or 'lack of class' or whatever fucking excuse he came up with until I would inevitably change my mind. Towards the end, when I tried to express myself, thinking that maybe it wasn't intentional...that perhaps we could work through it...he just became worse."

The chill of the night air has done nothing to cool the raging heat inside of me. *How can anyone have this divine creature in their hands and not worship her? None the less have the audacity to restrain her? Try to make her into something else? Who would dare keep a treasure like Celeste, the true Celeste, from the light?* I try to calm myself before I speak, so that my anger doesn't come off in my tone with her. "Worse how?"

She whips towards me, eyes wide. *Shit, maybe I didn't manage to keep it out of my tone as well as I'd hoped.* "He didn't hit me or anything. I don't mean that! He just..." She looks down again, almost as if she's ashamed. "He got *mean*. Like viciously cruel in his words and not trying to hide it at all. I'd be backed into a corner, face-to-face with him, screaming about wasting time on me. How I was a classless whore that he'd thought would grow out of these silly interests. How I was from a respectable family and yet I wanted to make myself a disgrace to them and to him. How I was selfish because what I did or how I looked reflected on all of them and I was more concerned with my fleeting shallow desires than their reputations or happiness."

Dabbing under her eyes with her sleeve, Celeste continues, "And the worst part is, I still didn't leave. I thought the problem was me and that I had driven this 'good' guy to be so unhappy he was lashing out. So I tried. I buried myself even deeper. But I still came home to him in bed with another woman, one that seemed to so easily be everything he had to force me to be. So I left and let him have her, while I went to finally go have myself. He didn't even argue with me. No excuses, no pleas, no regrets. We both just went on with our lives."

Fucking bastard. No wonder she stayed single so long and still has trust issues. All abuse is horrible, but emotional wounds take a lot longer to heal than a bruise. I'm surprised she tries with me at all...hell why does she? But as much as that question is burning in my mind, I don't ask her because this isn't about me, or even us. This is about Celeste and I'm here for her tonight. I finally get a chance to sit by her side and comfort her as she faces all the demons in her head.

"I know you're probably going to roll your eyes at me, but he's an idiot, and sounds like a narcissist as well. You are *not* responsible for how other people react to you. You do not need to police yourself for anyone's comfort or happiness but your own. You. Are. *Amazing.* Celeste, I'm sorry for all the people in your life that didn't see it. But I do, so do your friends, but in the end, we don't matter either. The person who needs to see it is *you*."

Instead of rolling, her eyes lock onto mine, a storm of emotion awash in them. The smeared tears on her cheek give her the same glow that you see in tragic Renaissance paintings.

She looks ethereal. "Damian," she whispers as she leans into me, kissing me once again.

This one is sweet and tender. From a place of emotion rather than lust. We meld together like one of the chemistry experiments she taught me how to do. Two separate elements, bonding to create an entirely new compound. *I will never let her go. I can't. She's a part of me now, as I am her.* The witch has made a potion of us, and this is the kind of magic that can't be undone.

Celeste

I'm laying in bed half asleep, dazed as I stare at the pool of moonlight streaming through the window onto my wall. April called me early this morning, desperate to talk it out over Issac and her decision to hide his inquiry from me. It wasn't an easy discussion, but we worked through it. Definitely a shitty way to start the day, though. Savannah waited until we worked together tonight to bring it up. I'm still upset , but I know they meant well. *Misguided and made a terrible call, but meant well.* It might've helped my forgiving attitude that they both stayed, I don't know how late, on Friday, cleaning up, so I could basically have Saturday to myself to process everything.

Though I spent most of it overanalyzing my discussion with Damian. I have no idea why I shared so much. *Yes, you do. Fucking spiked cider.* Yet as much as I'd like to blame the alcohol, it was *more* than that. It is so easy and natural with him. I *wanted* to open up and share my pain. And that fucking terrifies me. *Stupid.* It's so early, I barely know him, and I don't have a great track record of picking people. It feels right...but I can't trust myself or what I want at this point.

Issac coming back out of the woodwork isn't helping those feelings either. *Really? Now?! When I finally try to pursue something again, he pops back up like a goddamn lesion.* I don't know what he wants, honestly I don't fucking care, but I can't shake the feeling that it's a sign from the universe about Damian and me. I just can't decide what it's trying to say.

Working last night, getting up early with April, and then bartending again tonight has me exhausted. My body should just shut down, but the paranoia and self-doubt is keeping my mind galloping in circles. Though I'm running on fumes, which is why I assume I dozed off without realizing it and didn't wake until it was far too late.

Gentle tugs on my wrists are the first sensations that register, disturbing my slumber. My body feels like it is made of stone, the weight of my limbs wearing on my joints. Instinctually, I go to roll over and readjust, needing to rub the sleep from my eyes, when they fly open with the sudden realization that I can't move my hands.

Above me, staring back from the mirrors on the ceiling, is a disheveled woman, with her hair splayed around her head, stretched naked over the black satin sheets with her wrists and ankles bound to each post of the bed with bright orange ribbon like a spooky little present. The curves of her body are on full display. Her large breasts, falling slightly to the sides with gravity, emphasize the smaller waist between them and her ample hips. Her limbs are pulled tight, arching her back and thrusting her chest into the air. The spread of her legs showing off her pussy lips from under the small tuft of hair on her mound. Her pale skin is reflecting the moonlight.

My pale skin is reflecting the moonlight.

I'm tied naked and spread eagle on my bed.

That's me...what the fuck is happening?

As I continue to rouse back into reality, the instinct to struggle finally comes to life. Pulling hard on the ties, I aggressively jerk my hands and feet until the ribbon digs into my skin. Even when I strain to the point of cutting off circulation to my limbs, the binds won't give. *Well, the bastard clearly knows how to tie a fucking knot.*

A clearing of the throat cutting through the silence makes me freeze. *Stupid. Of course he's still here and watching.* I strain my neck to look down past my body, where I discover him standing between the two posts at the end of my bed. A hand resting on each, waiting patiently as he enjoys the view of my bare flesh, splayed and on display for him. The mask may hide his eyes, but I can feel them on my body, devouring me. He's shirtless, wearing only the disguise, gloves, and dark jeans yet again. But even in the dim light, I can see his cock straining against the confines of his pants already. I wonder if he can see the moisture collecting along my pussy lips from the mere sight of him. *Fuck. What has this psycho done to me?*

The new mattress is silent and hardly shifts with his weight as he climbs onto the bed, sitting sideways between my legs. *Damn, no wonder I didn't wake up sooner.* His gloved hand reaches out, running along my bare skin, from ankle to inner thigh - slowly, methodically. I don't dare to shift or fight, for the fear that any sudden movement might startle the beast out of him. *I've never been as vulnerable to him as I am now...and yet that realization just makes me wetter.* My body is already on the verge of trembling and he's barely touched me.

His fingers reach my pussy, gliding along the lips, collecting my glistening juices on the leather. I gasp, causing him to break out in a smile that flashes menacingly in the moonlight. *Wait...smile?* That's when I see it. He's removed the netting from the twisted mouth of the mask, unveiling a break in the latex large enough to see his teeth and most of his lips. It only makes the mask more unsettling. A demon pumpkin sporting a mouth full of human teeth that could rip me apart...especially when I'm laid out helplessly like a three course meal...*shiver-inducing.*

As if he can read my mind, he lifts the glove to his face, slipping his tongue through the mouth of the mask and licks it clean. "Mmmm, I knew there was a reason I called you my Sweet. You are delicious."

My pussy pulses with his words, as if begging for me to let him taste more of it. The mask's voice changer is still altering his true sound, but without the netting, it is less effective. He barely sounds demonic...*maybe even familiar?*

But before I get a chance to really contemplate what I'm hearing, he is crawling over my body, brushing his bare chest against every inch of my prickling skin as he works his way up to my face. I can feel his hot exhales on my chest and then my neck as his hands explore all the tender parts of me. My breath catches and I forget how to breathe. Not from fear, not from panic, but from pure lust. *I want this man to eat me alive. I can't deny it anymore. I might hate myself in the morning, but I want this.* His tongue darts out from the mask and trails up the length of my neck, until he reaches my ear and lets out a satisfied groan at the taste of me.

Again, my pussy spasms. *The effect he has on me is insane...maybe I'm just as unstable as he is.* He sits up on me, sliding one hand slowly over my stomach, between my breasts, and over my chest until it lays softly, but possessively around my throat.

His grip twitches, squeezing for only a second before releasing again. But it must have been enough to make my eyes startle, because he lets out a deep, mischievous chuckle.

"What's wrong, Witch? Afraid you might finally reap what you've sown?" He does it again, squeezing tight enough on each side of my throat to trap my breath for a couple seconds before relaxing his grip.

My stomach tightens. *Did he see Damian and me? Does he know?* I gasp out, "I didn't do anything to you." I try to make it sassy, to give it a touch of spite, but it comes out breathy and desperate. The same way he is making my pussy feel.

"Oh, but you did, my Sweet. You put a spell on me with these lips..." the fingers of his other hand trace over them lightly, before falling to my side and running along my curves. "With this body."

Trembling, I stare back into those soulless black orbs, searching for anything. Even with the relief at knowing this isn't about Damian, I can't relax. I feel like a plaything while bound and in his hands...*and I love and hate it.* My juices are running down from my pussy into my ass crack as he teases me because I'm unable to close my legs. My scent is filling the air and I am very aware that he must know what he's doing to me. That knowledge only makes the situation worse, causing me to blush and grow even wetter.

His hand tightens against the sides of my throat again, toying with my breath. Those black voids never leave my vision as he makes me gasp and struggle for air before loosening his grip. "You took my breath away from the first moment we met. Why shouldn't you experience the same thing?"

When I try to snap back at him, he squeezes again, cutting off my reply. The mask tilts slowly to the side as he stares at me, like a cat that's caught a mouse and can't decide whether it should eat it or play with it. He groans as I test the strength of the binds once more and buck my naked body against him, his hard cock grinding on me through his jeans.

I'm straining for air against his grip, pulling in ragged breaths. But even though I'm managing to breathe, I'm still getting lightheaded. He isn't putting any pressure on the front of my throat or windpipe, but the tension on the sides is restricting blood flow. My body is breaking out in tingles, *dangerous and delicious.* Fingers twitching, pussy convulsing, and mouth fallen open in a desperate need, I am losing myself in his warped pleasures. His smile is toothy and menacing through the mouth of the mask, making me shiver in his hold as my eyes start to flutter.

Immediately, he releases my throat and grinds harder against me. My body floods with sensations similar to release, causing it to shake as I moan. His jeans are rough, but stimulating on my clit, making me yell out louder in pleasure as I gasp for air. A satisfied, smug chuckle escapes him. "Such a good, needy little witch. I love the way your body responds to me."

His gloved hand slides down between us, flying straight to my clit and rubbing hard, making my back bend sharply and the ribbons pull tight as I cry out passionately. This time, after slipping a finger gently into my folds to coat it, he brings it to my lips, painting my juices onto them like lipstick before shoving his finger into my mouth. The taste of leather and my sweetness permeates my tongue. I suck hard, giving into every deviant desire he brings to life inside me.

A growl rumbles from deep in his chest as I pull his finger farther into my mouth. I can feel his cock twitch from it. *Brag all you want about what you do to my body, but yours is just as affected by me.* He has to fight me to get his finger back out. I bite hard, trying to keep it there, making him grunt and snatch his hand back. The lust is apparent in the raspiness of his voice as he replies, "Taking your breath away because you took mine first wasn't enough of a lesson, my Sweet? You thought biting me would have no consequences?" His voice drops, "Or did you just want to be eaten alive that badly, Witch?"

He reaches past me to my nightstand and collects one last piece of ribbon. He places it tightly over my eyes and lifts me into his chest as he knots it behind my head, blindfolding me. The sudden loss of my sight makes me pay more attention to all my other senses. The smell of his skin is intoxicating. *Go to the grave as annoying as possible.* I bite into his chest, giggling as the muscle flexes beneath my teeth, his reactive groan is erotic and sends chills down my spine.

"Very well, Witch, who am I to deny you what you clearly need," his mouth moves right beside my ear, warm breath washing over me. Even with his voice as quiet and soft as possible with that voice changer, his next words make me chill. "Just remember, you cast the spell that made me obsessed with you. I am your punishment for practicing witchcraft, my Sweet. I'm here to break your walls and release that dark divine creature inside you, just as you set mine free."

His words dance in my head as he slides down my body. I see colors in the lids of my closed eyes that move with the rhythm of his tongue against my skin. He's taking his time working his way along my neck and chest. *Savoring me.* Pausing between my breasts, he takes first one nipple and then the other into his mouth, lavashing them with attention. My moans fill the room. Electricity is running through my body, directly from my breasts to my pussy. *God, I'm already close.*

I feel the pricking before I piece together what is happening. A sharp sting strikes in the tender space between my breasts, followed quickly by an immense pressure that has me yelling out and moaning in a mix of pain and pleasure. *He fucking bit me back.* And now he's sucking hard on the sensitive spot making me writhe in the intense sensations. *Fuck, I hope he sucks a clit like that.* Every pull of his suction makes my pussy clenches in response. My body is desperate for release...desperate for *him*.

A smug chuckle drowns out my moan. "Look at that, now you have such a pretty little witch's mark." *He gave me a hickey on my chest? Fuck.*

I groan as his attention continues down my bare flesh, over my stomach and to my mound, leaving behind trails of moisture cooling on my skin. His strong hands are digging into my thighs with a barely contained need. *It is taking everything he has to resist ravaging me right now. I can tell...but do I want him to?* My body certainly doesn't. I have no desire to say "trick" and end this game. But if he plans to fuck me...am I going to let him?

His breath washes over my soaking pussy and my mind goes white. I have no thought or care other than the need that is radiating from between my thighs, begging for him to make me cum. The moment his tongue glides along my slit, I spasm, straining against my binds and practically panting.

I look desperate and wild, *and I don't care*. This is what I *want*, what I *crave*, and I refuse to be ashamed of it anymore. Breathlessly, I whisper, "Please..."

Next thing I know, his mouth is wrapped around my clit and I am screaming in pleasure. His tongue is melting me in all the best ways, with the tip perfectly pressed against me, massaging as he sucks on my sweet button. My juices must be coating his fucking mask. The latex is slick between my thighs, sticking to me slightly, but I can't be bothered to care. Not when he's devouring the soul from my body. His tongue dips into me making me spasm, "Oh fuck...yes!"

He can have me. All of me. As long as he doesn't stop.

I'm delirious with pleasure, lost in the symphony he's playing with my senses. Feeling his hands on my curves while he sets every nerve on fire with his mouth on my pussy, the sounds of his groans as he eats me, and the scent of his body mixed with my arousal has me rocketing towards my release.

"Celeste..." He groans my name as he presses two fingers into my tight, soaking pussy. They slip in easily with all the lubrication and he immediately flips them up and hooks me, massaging inside as he latches down onto my clit again. I throw my head back like a fucking possesed woman as I thrash in pleasure.

The combination throws me over the edge and I am screaming in my release. My entire body is tingling and spasming in his hands but he doesn't slow. The suction continues as he forces me to ride out my orgasm on his fingers and I know I must be soaking him. My fingers knot around the ribbons as I pull harder against them. I can feel my breasts swaying from the strength of my spasms. My yells must be carrying across the fields, I'm screaming so loud.

I barely hear him over myself, "Yes, my Sweet. You are magnificent. Scream for me."

Sweat has broken out over my entire body by the time my orgasm subsides and I collapse against the bed. The air chills the moisture as I calm, coming down from the mind shattering pleasure I just experienced.

I have never cum like that before. And I just let a stranger...a fucking stalker...do that to me. But as much as I know I should care...*I don't. It was delicious, dark, and everything I have wanted for so long...whether I should want it doesn't matter now. Because now that I've had it, I know I can never go back.*

Damian

Walking away from a beautifully bound, quivering, and panting Celeste was the hardest thing I have ever done in my life. Forget fist fights, torture, *hell, even being shot.* None of it compares to the physical pain it caused me to walk out and leave her begging for more, while my body was literally ravenous for her. No bloodlust I have ever had compared to the pure need I was suffering from to have that tight pretty pussy wrapped around myself.

Sticking to my plan and not giving into the calls of her body was the greatest feat of self control I have ever had. *And I kinda hate myself for it.* But I didn't eat a single caramel on the way home. I wasn't ready to lose the taste of her on my tongue yet.

Though I *did* have to stand in the corn and jerk off while watching her on the cameras before riding back home. There was no way I was going to straddle a bike for twenty minutes while dealing with blue balls like that. *Not that it took much.* I almost came while I was eating her out. *Celeste tastes fucking divine.* I cut one hand loose and abandoned her to untie herself as I quickly took off after she came on my lips. If I hadn't left *that* *moment* I would've ended up fucking her. *No doubts there.*

Even in the corn, it took all I had not to storm right back into that house and spread her legs again just so I could make her cum on my cock the same way. Watching her lay in that bed, naked, panting - so satisfied and exhausted that she couldn't even start to untie herself yet - made me practically feral with need.

There lies my Sweet.

My pretty little mess.

Mine.

I came so hard my knees went weak. *I'm screwed the first time I actually fuck her. Hell, maybe I'll be the one seeing stars.* That thought had a smile on my face the entire ride home. However, what I didn't know was that my self control was going to be tested in an entirely different way the next night and it would be...*almost* as hard to restrain myself.

Celeste will be home any minute. I've never been in her house three nights in a row before...*well never when she's also been in it at the same time.* This isn't part of the plan, but I can't stay away. I'm craving the taste of her again already. *I'm practically a mad man.* I've relieved myself four times throughout the day and I am still unable to resist the urge to come see her. I don't know what I'm actually doing...*I haven't really thought this through, but eating her out until she cums like that again certainly can't hurt my cause.*

The rumble of car wheels on the gravel announces her arrival and I press closer to the wall outside of the bedroom window. Her headlights bounce with the car as it moves over the rocks and washes over the front of the porch. *Should I make a move out here? I mean, I might have to chase her through the corn but, fuck, that could be fun.* I'm busy picturing exactly what the cold air and the adrenaline of a chase would do to her nipples, when she climbs out of her car and I realize she's on the phone.

"--Accusing you or Eric of anything, but he doesn't fucking know anyone else in my life, so if you guys didn't tell him where to find me, that's even scarier!" She's practically yelling into the phone, storming up the steps. But she doesn't head inside once she's on the porch.

Oh fuck. Don't come around this side. The pause in her stride has me considering a panicked nosedive over the railing and an army crawl into the stalks. However, my reprieve arrives with the renewed sounds of her steps heading the other direction and the creak of the porch swing as she takes a seat.

"It's not the same, April! That 'real' stalker hasn't hurt me like Issac has. Some random guy in this small town figuring out where I live over god knows how long is less alarming than Issac showing up at my fucking job when he just decided to ask about me last week." The discomfort in her voice is apparent.

Rage floods me, replacing all the horniness I had for Celeste with a bloodlust for that piece of shit. *How dare he?* Suddenly, it isn't her guts I want to be in.

Her voice catches my attention again, "I don't even know what he wants from me. He just strolled into Juke's like nothing ever happened and it hasn't been four years, sits down, and tries to start a conversation. It was crazy." The creaks of the swing start to pick up as her nerves make her twitchier. The impulse to go wrap my arms around her like I did the other night on the porch hits me like a truck...but I can't. *In this mask, I'm not Damian to her. I'm not her comfort...but I can be her vengeance if she wants me to be.*

The words are rapidly tumbling from her, "He started on how it was nice to see me, as if it was a fucking accident and he didn't clearly hunt me down, and then quickly shifted to how life's treating him, I guess bragging or some shit? I don't know. But *then* he moved into his whole underhanded compliments shit, insulting and demeaning me while acting like it's actually something sweet, you know?"

He insulted her? I'll rip his fucking tongue out and then feed it back to him. Who does he think he is to speak to this witch, none the less the audacity to insult *her?*

She pauses for a moment before replying, "She was in the back changing out a keg when he first came in, but as soon as she saw me fucking shaking like a leaf when she returned she intervened, but it was embarrassing. I can't believe I fucking let him see that he can still upset me like that." *There she goes again. Holding herself responsible for too much...I wonder if she'd blame herself if I laid his body at her feet...or would that darkness inside her revel in it?*

Her breath is ragged, like she's fighting tears. *Making Celeste cry from pain...true pain is a fucking sin. Absolutely damnable.* My mother's deranged tirades come to mind again. *The guilty can't outrun damnation, Damian. God knows all. No one escapes judgement. One way or another, they all end up burning in hell like they deserve.* That red rage that overtakes me is making my blood pound in my veins. *If Isasac was here right now, I'd probably beat him past the point of identification with my bare fucking hands.*

Actually, imagining the sounds of his face shattering beneath my fist and the sting of my knuckles being soothed by the heat of his blood all over them helps the red-hot flames recede from my body...*some.*

"I guess...I don't know, April, I just..." she pauses and breathes deep. "I felt weak and I fucking hate that. Even when the cook made him leave, he had the fucking gall to write his number down on a napkin first. Does he really believe that he can just have me back? This bastard really thinks, what? That he left me and I've just been waiting?"

She groans, getting up from the swing. I hear her keys jingling as she makes her way back to the door. "Either way, I've got to try and get some sleep. I'm exhausted and I have a lot of shit on my mind. But I wanted to tell you he came by."

It was then that I decided to leave her be tonight, no matter how tempting the idea of *distracting* her was. She's not in a place for our games this evening and it isn't her fault. So instead, I'll spend my night doing some research and planning something new for our seasonal...escapades. *Get some rest, my Sweet. He won't be bothering you for long, I promise.*

Celeste

The fields are passing by too quickly as I make my way to campus today. I'm going to see Damian in class and I'm *dreading* it. Even Osiris could tell I've been unusually stressed and agitated since Sunday. He's been extra attentive and cuddly. But if he knew I was messing stuff up with his new buddy he'd probably ostracize me.

Everything was perfect Friday night. If I was a normal woman we would be well on our way to a fabulous relationship with this amazing story to tell everyone about how we met. *But no, instead I have to be a fucked up, horny, mentally ill woman who enjoys her stalker's unhinged behavior.*

All I've been thinking about since that fucking pumpkin plague left my house was what I was going to say to Damian. I don't know what to do. I *really* care about him and our chemistry is incredible. He's sexy, charming, handy, understanding, a great listener, and a killer kisser...but our night together didn't keep me from folding to every sensation my stalker brought out in me. And deep down...*I can't deny that it won't stop me from doing it again.*

You know the right thing to do, Celeste. My stomach knots up so tight that acid rushes up my throat. I revolt from the acrid taste in the back of my mouth just as much as I do from the thought. *You know what Issac's cheating did to you. You are not going to be a selfish bitch and do the same to Damian. He deserves better.* It's the truth. The idea of hurting him makes me tear up. But so does the thought of letting him go.

I understand we just started dating and we didn't really know each other well before that, but I haven't felt this way about someone in so long - hopeful. I'm not delusional. We aren't in love yet...but I think we could end up that way. I feel safe, seen, and valued with Damian. It's all I've ever really needed in life...and it's also what I've never really had. He could be my perfect match, but if I can't give him what he deserves in return, then I have no right to him. *And for some reason, I doubt being a plaything to a pumpkin-faced stalker is on his dream girl checklist.*

I pull into a space and park, laying my head down on the steering wheel so I won't risk seeing him walk into the building and just take off in the other direction. *I can stare down and sass a fucking stalker with a knife no problem, but a break up? Nope. Where is the emergency exit please?*

The neon numbers on my dash feel like the countdown on a fucking bomb. I push it until there is only ten minutes before class and I have no choice but to head inside. *You could call in sick to Professor Beck…damn it. If only I'd fucking thought of that earlier this morning.* Instead, I'm about to spend the next two to three hours overseeing lab experiments in the same room as Damian while holding this all in until the end of class? *Shit.*

The rocks that drop in my stomach make it immediately clear I'm not going to be able to manage that. This will have to be done before class if I have a chance at functioning properly. *I'm sure that's just going to be peachy.* I steel myself, unwilling to let my personal emotions interfere with my work. *Ha, good luck with that.* I'm already sweating in the high neck t-shirt I had to wear to hide the fucking hickey.

When I reach the lab, my eyes find him immediately. He was perched on his stool watching the door and broke out into that charming smile the moment I entered the room. *Destroying that is going to kill me.* I lay my bag at my desk before walking over and attempting to subtly ask, "Mr. LaCroix, can I see you in the hallway please?"

However, the subtleness did not stop the class from breaking out into a low chorus of, "Ohhhs," as if we were all back in elementary school and he was being sent to the principal's office. *Children. The entire lot of them. Today is* not *the day.* Damian isn't much better though, giving me suggestive eyebrows before I spin on my heels and lead the way from the classroom.

As soon as we are out of earshot he starts to speak, "I don't know what I did, *Ms. Carroll,* but if you're going to paddle me, you left the ruler behind on the desk. I can go -"

When I turn to face him, I can't hide the tears collecting in my eyes and his entire demeanor changes. Immediately, he steps closer and lifts my chin with one hand while he brushes my hair back with the other.

"Celeste, what's wrong? What's going on?" His beautiful, fiery eyes search mine intensely with real concern. *He cares. Really cares. Fuck me and my sick shit. Goddamn it.*

I slowly reach up and wrap my hands around his wrists, pulling them away from me. Stepping back, I look down, unable to meet his gaze, "Damian, we need to talk."

He lets out a small, nervous laugh, "Well, no man likes to hear those words." His pulse is pounding beneath my grip.

"Friday was incredible, and I want to thank you for listening to me. I know that was a lot of heavy stuff to drop on you so soon, and you were very kind, but I don't think this is going to wor-"

"Is this about Issac? Did he do something? Celeste, I'm not worried about-"

"No!" I step back and let go of him. I'm embarrassed at my outburst, but every second we do this, the harder it is not to implode. All I *want* is to wrap myself in his arms and tell him everything. About my stalker, my predilections, my dreams, and my nightmares; he makes me want to share *everything*. But he'd reject me like *any sane man would* and I don't think I could recover from that. It'd end up with me dying alone as a crazy old lady with my only companion being a stuffed Osiris.

At least this way I can always pretend, "what if".

"Damian...it's not about anyone but me. You are amazing, but I'm just not ready for a relationship yet." I finally get the guts to meet his eyes and I wish I hadn't.

They are roiling with...rage? Pain? I can't tell exactly but it *isn't* pleasant. Like molten lava ready to destroy everything in its path. Yet somehow, his voice comes out steady and calm. "You certainly seemed ready on Friday."

Wow. Dick. "Don't be like that. We just started dating. This wasn't serious yet. I know we have chemistry, Damian, and I'm sorry. *I really am.* But I can't do this."

He breaks our stare, looking up at the ceiling, licking his lip and nodding his head. "You're right. Nothing that serious. Just some kisses and a couple hallmark dates. Probably the romance of the moments more than anything." Dropping his gaze back to mine he continues, "Right, Celeste?"

No. "Yeah."

He shoves his fists back into his pant's pockets, looking at anything but me at this point. "Got it... Um. I'm going to go ahead and head out, Ms. Carroll. I've had some personal stuff come up and I'm not able to participate in lab today." He whirls around and storms back into the class to collect his belongings.

The tears overrun, racing down my cheeks. *Fuck, I wish I could just ditch too.*

Damian

Don't do it. Not yet. The urge to beat something is racing through my veins. *Make it to the truck.* I'm practically running from the building to the parking lot. *Desperate* to get to my own space before I explode and take who knows who out with me when I do.

What the fuck is she thinking.

I love *her.*

Sure, I haven't said it yet, but she has to be able to feel it.

The parking lot is empty, everyone who would bother to be here is currently sitting in a class. *Good.* If some jackass bumped into me right now, we'd both end up spending the rest of our week somewhere unpleasant - a hospital for him and jail for me. I hurry across the pavement and jump into the cab of the truck.

As soon as the door closes behind me, my fists are pummeling into the steering wheel. Each fresh sting of pain from the impact makes my mind a little clearer. I don't know exactly how long I sat there, swinging the rage out of my body. *No. Not rage...fear.* I've had rage for a long time and it certainly can make me lash out, but never *uncontrollably so.* I always choose when to let it out. I can turn the violence on and off like a faucet when it is rage...but fear? That's not normal for me. I don't get scared often. When I do, that's when I lose control. Like on the day Kage threatened Celeste...I was angry, sure, but I was terrified as well.

As much as I *hate* to admit it, she makes me vulnerable to fear. I may be the one that stalks and chases her in the night, who spent almost a year planning how to scare her panties off, but she can terrify me without even trying. And to be honest... *I have no idea what to do with that.*

I don't know why she would do this. Everything has been going so *well*. Our games are clearly satisfying her and our dates have been almost nauseatingly storybook. *We are perfect for each other. She has been opening up to me, emotionally and sexually. Hell, she's been opening up to herself! That dark, divine goddess she represses has been emerging...and she loves it.* So what the fuck is happening? How could she not want me? *Us?* Who in their right mind would walk away from what we have?

"This wasn't serious yet." Her voice echoes in my head and makes my blood cold and thick in my veins. *She didn't mean that. She doesn't know what she's saying. Clearly, she's under some kind of duress and it's causing her to make poor choices. She* can *love you. You felt it in her kiss. You have ever since the first one at that party.*

Issac. None of this started until after Issac showed back up in her life. *I can take care of that.*

There's no need to start plotting her kidnapping...yet. Just keep with the new plan and see where this goes. If she still rejects you *after* the next first quarter moon, *then* you can start looking for remote properties out in the midwest.

Celeste

I'm conducting one last outfit check in my mirror when I hear Savannah pull into the drive. Ever since I broke it off with Damian over a week ago, I've been absolutely miserable. He didn't show up to lab this week either. *If he fails this class over me I'm never going to forgive myself.* Not to mention that my stalker has also been MIA since our last...encounter. I swear to god if trying to be a good person cost me a fabulous man just for me to never see this masked stranger again, I'm going to implode. *It's just karma for being such a needy degenerate, Celeste. You can't complain.* Ugh.

But I'd have felt guiltier if I had kept seeing him after I came the way I did with my stalker. I know I didn't ask for it...but I also didn't use the safe word to stop it either. *Yes,* Damian and I weren't exclusive or anything, so it wasn't technically cheating...yet. But I've come to realize I *really* enjoy my masked man's games and I'm not going to be able to resist him. Damian deserves better than that, and I care about him enough not to hurt him, so I can be selfish. Just because I harbor feelings for him while I suffer from an unhinged, feral lust for another man, doesn't mean I get to have both. *Still fucking hurts, though.*

The darker part of my mind was also hoping that *maybe* my stalker would catch Issac trying to reach back out to me and get territorial. Perhaps take out all that aggression on him...for real. I'd much rather Issac be at risk than Damian. That asshole has it coming. A disgusted shiver runs down my spine as I think back to the way he leered at me when he strolled into Juke's last Monday night.

"Damn, Cee, you're looking good. If I knew you were going to pull off all that trashy shit like a porn star, I wouldn't have fought you so hard about it." His voice, which used to sound so smooth to me, just felt like slime sliding down my skin. The cadence of it made me feel *dirty*.

It was only Savannah running interference and the insistence of the cook that Issac leave after I had to run to the kitchen to get the shaking under control that made me able to finish my shift that night. But his perfect fucking teeth, ironed polo, and vicious eyes have been haunting me since. I swear I've caught sight of him outside of the bar a few times over the last two weeks, but he's always gone before anyone else can witness it. *What the fuck am I? Stalker bait?*

Hell if he maimed him, I might even be tempted to show my appreciation very enthusiastically after. But as my luck would have it, Pumpkin Face has up and disappeared right when I could actually use his obsession for more than an adrenaline rush and an orgasm.

However, I have tickets to Wraithhill Trails tonight to start October out with a bang, and I am determined to enjoy myself. It isn't the fanciest, tech-heavy haunt, but it's fucking huge and quality. It's one of the largest in the southeast and they are dedicated to the scares. Tickets are limited each night and they sell out most of the time. When you first arrive, they put everyone on a tram and take you through the forest to the top of the hill. Then they break you into smaller groups, of about four or five, that they send into the haunt at five minute intervals. From there, your group has to navigate the trails down the hill through the woods, with only a single lantern to guide the way. They even ask guests to leave their cellphones in their cars or in a locker. If you get caught using a light other than the lantern, then you can get a lifetime ban. The trail would probably take half an hour on its own in the dark, but add in dead end paths and a ton of scare actors who chase you around and suddenly you are easily looking at an hour to ninety minute experience. I try to milk it for every second I can get each year.

I used to work as a scare actor there when I was in college and I fucking loved it. Of course the seasonals have insane turn over, so most of the current actors don't know me personally, but after working four seasons in a row, the year-round employees and show managers all remember me. Which has its perks, like still being given the employee discount on concessions and merch, but my favorite is the more intense experience. When the managers clock me, they always take a moment to say hi and then get on the radios to give the actors a description of my outfit and my name along with a code "pitch black".

Haunt performers are already trained to look for the right "mark". If you can get one person in the group panicky, it will spread to the rest eventually. There are the obvious signs, like hiding behind other people or clinging to someone else's hand or arm, but also sweet and bright clothing, hair, makeup, or energies can highlight you as a prime target. The hardcore fans, the ones that are here just to watch their friends suffer, tend to dress more like the actors themselves. But there are rules, such as you never chase someone out of your boundaries or actually touch a visitor. A "pitch black" experience is saved for exclusive guests that the managers know *want* and *can* endure a more extreme experience. It means all the rules are out the window. But just because I'm a masochist, I dress to look like a prime mark as well. You know, in case someone missed the memo...or to see if I can make the actors twice as feral.

Savannah's seen some crazy shit happen when she's gone with me. April refuses to ever come back, but that's probably for the best. I thought she might actually have a heart attack when the guy with the chainsaw had me backed against a tree and put it between my legs. Savannah and I have to warn people who end up in our group now, because one year the other guests tried to file complaints about the number of masked actors who put their hands on me. *That was a damn good year.*

I've made an art out of catching the performers' attention. This used to be the only night of the year I got to indulge in my mask kink and it needed to be good enough to sustain me until the next October, so I've always done what I can to help. I curl my hair and put so much highlighter on my face and breasts, that even the dim lantern reflects off them. It's also always a small, bright dress with some "cute" accessory to make it appear that I'm a normie who is trying to be fun and festive to fit the vibe. This year is a tight, white, v-neck body con dress, paired with a mini wings harness, a cross necklace, and halo hair clip. No panties or bra, so I don't have to worry about the underwear lines messing with the aesthetic. I'm going into the lion's den dressed like a lamb and it *works*.

Though apparently I've gotten too good at catching masked men's attention. Now I've got one that followed me home. Two small beeps interrupt my thoughts, as Savannah lets me know she's ready to leave. I do one last spin before I head out, admiring how the dress clings to all my curves in the best ways. *Forget Damian, Issac, and Pumpkin Face, tonight is for me and I'm going to fucking enjoy it.*

"The no bra was a solid choice, those guys aren't going to be able to leave you alone. Hell, I'm your friend and I'm having a hard time keeping my eyes off them." Savannah is whispering in my ear while we wait for our turn to enter the trail, and we both laugh as the man at the gate keeps proving her point. His gaze repeatedly bouncing from his watch to my nipples and back again like a game of pong. The cold have made them very visible through the white fabric, straining against the confines of the dress's cups and looking especially lascivious on either side of the ornate cross. Savannah's right, I'm going to have a blast running from all the men tonight.

We've been paired with a random teenage couple, which concerned me at first but they both look like they're haunt regulars. She's even wearing a Wraithhill Trails merch shirt from last year. She also started bouncing when we explained to them that I was on a pitch black call and stuff might get a little crazy. The guy seemed hesitant at first, but once Savannah explained it doesn't mean anyone is going to touch them more than normal, just that they will see the actors do some wild shit to me, he was all on board. *Budding voyeur right there.*

"Okay y'all, step up to the gate," Pong Eyes calls out to us as he collects an electric lantern from the crates behind him. Turning it on and handing it to Savannah, he continues with his spiel, "Any additional forms of light, including but not limited to cellphones and flashlights, will result in removal from the attraction and a possible ban. The actors will not touch you," his eyes dart over to me, "well most of you. So do not touch them. Period. Touching an actor will result in removal from the attraction and a possible ban. Please *do* scream, squeal, and panic, however, remember to watch your step and if there is an actual emergency call a code red and any actor in the area will break character to assist you. Do not, *for any reason*, unless escorted by an employee in the case of an emergency, leave the paths. These woods are thick and you could easily get turned around in them. As much as we'd like to believe we are the scary things in the dark, we can not control what wildlife you may run into if you get lost out there." He pushes the gate, letting it swing open with a creak as he drops his voice dramatically and steps out of the way, "Now enjoy your trip through Wraithhill Trails and we will see you on the other side...of either the path or life."

I can't help the giddy smile that overtakes my face as I skip off into the inky darkness of the night. Natural debris crunches under my shoes as I make my way down the path, Savannah laughing right behind me, and the couple hand in hand bringing up the rear. This part of the haunt is dense with webs and spiders in the trees, suspended over the trail. I catch a glimpse of movement off to the left as we approach the first fork.

I spin around, practically high from the excitement and giggling. "Which way guys?"

The small girl in the back replies first, "Either is fine with me!"

"Why don't you just lead the way, Cee, and if anyone else has an opinion they can pipe up then? Otherwise you're going to do this at every break in the path," she sighs. Turning to the teens she continues, "Even when we are running from a guy with a chainsaw she'll want to check if y'all are okay with where she's headed first. For someone who loves horror movies so much, she'd probably die in a real one."

I haven't yet.

"Yeah, don't worry about us. We are going to follow you...and run when you run." The girl's laugh fills the air and *almost* covers the sound of a stick breaking off to the left. *Here we go.*

"Okay, then let's head left!" I announce loudly as I lead us into the first horror of the night.

The breeze causes the webs to sway gently in the air, the scent of moist earth carried with it. Savannah has the lantern held high, but the light only makes a dim sphere of illumination around us. The dense trees on either side of the path are still walls of impenetrable darkness. My pulse quickens. This is what I crave. The anticipation. *The fear of the unknown.* It floods my system with adrenaline, just like the people who are crazy about roller coasters or mountain climbing, this is my hit. It makes my body come alive. *Is this why I play the way I do with my stalker? Am I a fucking addict, doing dangerous shit just for the high?*

When we hear a muffled cry and the sounds of someone struggling in the brush, we all slow to a tiptoe, creeping closer to that side of the path. The light glides over a massive web until it reveals a girl bound in the center of it, fully cocooned other than her eyes and the hands trapped by her side. She's struggling so hard the lattice is disturbing the foliage under her, eyes wide with panic as she tries to scream through the web gag, hands shaking frantically. *She's good.*

I expect the scream from behind me before it happens. An attention-grabbing actor in the open is usually a distraction for another one to flank the group for a scare. *It worked.* The teenage boy shrieked so loud that I'm sure people back at the path entrance heard him. I whirl around to find a spider-human monstrosity towering over the group, a good eight feet tall. Four long legs, each attached to where a limb should be, stretch to the ground and bear his weight, while another four are raised and posed in the air. His face is painted thickly in black and white, dripping chelicerae attached to his sharp jaw. The paint continues down over his chest and stomach making ornate designs. *Fuck.*

Savannah squeals and steps back, casting the glow of the lantern over me. His head turns slowly to the side as I watch his eyes light up with recognition. My hand trembles. He smiles wide, unsettlingly wide, as he jolts one step forward, hunched further over on his front arms. *Is he really going to scurry on all four in stilts?* The couple and Savannah shuffle further back down the path, leaving me out in the open like bait...just how I like it.

"Cee...now is not the time to play fucking Miss Muffet. Come on." Savannah rushes out. *Damn, you know he's good if she's getting jumpy.* He scurries forward in a sudden burst before stopping again, enjoying the way we all jumped.

"Ohhhhh, Ceeeeeee," he drawls out his words in a singsong voice, "you look good enough to eat." His eyes dance down over my body, lingering on my chest. My breath catches, but not in the same way it would've a year ago. Then I would've been practically panting from the excitement of *this* man chasing me, living out a taste of my darker fantasies. But when he says "eat" all I can see in my mind is that damn demon pumpkin between my thighs, glistening with my juices which makes my heart race faster than anything on this trail ever has.

I take one step back on the path, still staring at the spider beast. That's all it took. Like a shark who smelled blood in the water, he takes off scurrying like an actual fucking spider, coming full speed at us.

"Run!" I spin on my heels and take off. I can hear him practically galloping after me. The group is ahead on the path, the light swinging wildly with Savannah's strides as the only point of reference while we make a break for it. The booms of his legs slamming into the dirt spurring us on. I'm catching up to the teens, about to overtake them when the sounds of his chase abruptly stops with a loud thud. *Strange.* But I don't dare to stop in case it's a trap.

I urge the teens to go faster until we bust into a little clearing where Savannah is waiting for us, bent over panting and mumbling about fucking spiders. Timidly, I peer back into the dark and I feel eyes trained on me. *Why is he stopping? Have we wandered into a new area already?* I squint, trying to notice anything around us. A broken-down wagon and some old farming tools litter the space but it's hard to see even in the open air. The moon is barely a sliver tonight as we are on the cusp of a new moon.

"Holy shit! That was crazy! This code pitch black shit is fucking cool!" The teenage girl is bubbling over, giddy with excitement. *I hope that kid doesn't mind wearing a costume, because she is definitely one of us mask-kink girlies.*

We are deeper into the attraction though, because there are four paths out of this clearing and you can hear echoes of screams and yells coming from all around. The cacophony of actors and guests carry over the woods clearly now that the sounds of our own heartbeats have receded from our ears. A cry of pain and a plea for help rings out from the path we came in on and something about it gives me a chill. A *real* one.

I turn toward one of the far exits out of the clearing. "Let's go guys, we need to keep moving."

But before we get halfway there, we hear cries coming from it. A group busts out of that same trail, into the clearing, screaming for their lives. "Don't go that way! It's a dead end and there's a fucking chainsaw dude!" They don't even slow down, throwing themselves onto the very next path in a hurry to find a way out. I glance down the trail, interest piqued by the chainsaw, but there's still a nagging feeling in my gut I can't shake. Instead, I turn to the third path and lead the group back into the woods that way.

In less than a minute, we are walking between two long collections of building facades, creating a ghost town with a giant, lit-up saloon in the middle of the road ahead, which will require you to pass through it of course. I thought I heard footsteps in the woods as we made our way in, but every time

I'd stop to listen it would only be drowned out by the deafening screams and the roar of power tools inside the saloon. Which would be enough to make most normal people's blood run cold, but that's not what makes the ice race along my veins at that moment.

That honor would belong to the sight of a pumpkin mask emerging from between two of the facades, tossing a familiar knife in the air, letting it spin before he catches it smoothly.

Chapter 16

Celeste

My pumpkin stalker is leaning against one of the porch posts, not bothering to look at us as he continues to toy with the blade. He's only wearing his mask, gloves, a leather vest, black pants, and his boots. The teenage girl lets out an impressed gasp. *Oh yeah, she's fucked up too.* I stop in place, the teens follow my lead, but Savannah keeps heading forward.

"Savannah, stop!" I hiss.

Her laugh cuts through the night, "Oh come on, after that spider-freak, what's a living gourd?" She turns towards him yelling, "What? Were her jack-o'-lanterns back home friends of yours?"

Something's different. I can't place my finger on whatever it is that is piquing my intuition, but I feel more at risk here - on this trail with other people around, than I ever have with him in my house. *Something about the energy around him feels* sharper *tonight. More dangerous.*

The deep reverberation of his voice changer makes me jump. "Maybe..." he pauses, turning his head slowly to look at me, shaking the knife in a way that is as familiar as his touch at this point. "Or maybe, I just have a debt to collect."

He can't be serious. He's fucking psycho. Showing up here?

"Ohhhhhh, scary," Savannah mocks, turning back at me with wide eyes. "Sounds like you're in trouble, Cee."

He pushes off the post fluidly, moving through the dark towards me. Savannah and these teenagers think this is just another pitch black experience. But he and I know better. My body knows better. I can't quite put a title to it, but there's an ice in the air that sinks deeper into me with every step he takes, closing the distance between us...*perhaps dread*? This doesn't feel like a game anymore.

Savannah steps out of his path, arms up in surrender. "I'm sorry, girl, but you're on your own with this one. I think you mutilated one too many relatives."

I can hear the smirk through the voice changer, "Consider me karma." The teenagers give him a wide berth, moving past me to join Savannah. He steps forward and places the tip of the blade under my chin, lifting it with the pressure of the point digging into my flesh.

Suddenly he seizes me with his other arm, whipping us around and trapping me against him, my back to his front. Leaving me staring helplessly out at my group with his blade to my throat as he whispers in my ear, his breath hot through the netting of the gnarled smile. "You are about to watch these people walk away and leave you alone to your fate with me, Celeste. *Because that's what this is.* Everything you are, everything you've done, has brought you to this point. All the witnesses to your tragedy believe it's just a silly game. They have no idea that you've gambled your soul to taste the darkness...and by the time they do, you will be too far gone, my Sweet. No one's coming to save you."

My breath catches. *I know he's right.* They are staring back at me, humor in their eyes. Savannah probably thinks I'm having the time of my life, why shouldn't she? This is what I beg for every visit. Hell, this is the level of shit I rave about all year long until I get a chance to take another hit. *All she sees is an addict getting her fix.* But with each step they take farther down the path from me, I feel like my lifeline to reality...to sanity...is slipping through my fingers.

"Wait, guys, wait for me." I hear myself speak, but it isn't urgent. It doesn't sound distressed, it barely comes out loud enough to be heard.

Savannah waves at me and winks, "I don't know, Cee, you look a little tied up at the moment. Have fun and I'll see you on the other side...of either the path or life." She mimics the voice of the gatekeeper before devolving into a mass of laughter with the couple as they all turn their backs on me and head towards the chaos of the saloon.

I feel him lean in close and breathe deep, *smelling* me. I've never felt so much like prey in my life. A chill runs down my spine, making my nipples strain against the dress even more and my pussy moisten. But as soon as he wraps both arms around me and lifts, carrying me backwards towards the set facades and off the path, all my survival instincts finally kick in. *If I go into those trees, I am not coming back out.* I can feel it in my gut.

Desperately I scream, "HELP! SOMEONE, PLEASE! SAVANNAH! DON'T LEAVE ME! No! Let me go, GODDAMN IT," Thrashing as hard as I can in his embrace, my frustration is building because I'm hardly able to move. My torso is pinned against him, making me melt as the heat of his body burns through my thin, flimsy dress. My upper arms are trapped beneath his bare, bulging muscles, keeping my hands by my side and against his thighs. I'm clawing desperately at his pants, trying to graze his balls.

My head is slamming violently back into his chest while my kicks connect with his shins. My screams echo off the trees, mixing with the cacophony of other squeals, yells, and cries, from the monsters and guests of the haunt alike. But he doesn't seem fazed, just continuing to carry me back into the darkness past all the set pieces and scaffolding. He's dragging me deeper into the forest. The light of Savannah's lantern is getting smaller, but I still hear their voices, so I know they should be able to hear me. "HELP ME! PLEASE! IT'S HI-" His gloved hand slams over my mouth.

"You can yell and plead all you want, my Sweet, but no one's going to care. These woods are reverberating with screams tonight and yours will be lost among all the others. I can do what I want with you. All you're going to accomplish with those pleas is making me cum faster."

My mouth jerks as I try to bite the hand that's clasped over it. He snatches it back quickly, letting my scream echo out again while his dark laugh mixes in the air with it. His hard cock is pressing into my ass as he carries me and it twitches in response to my yell. *Bastard. Fuck him and this sick shit.* It's at that moment that I remember our first night together. "Trick". *One word and this all stops, Celeste.*

Suddenly he turns, dropping me over a sheet of wood that's balanced across two sawhorses. My thighs are pressed against it, just below the hem of my dress, so my bare skin is pillowing around the rough edges as he presses into me, bending us forward. He keeps one hand wrapped around my arms and torso, as the other grabs my chin roughly.

"You came traipsing into these woods dressed as a *fucking angel* while clearly begging for the attention of *more* masked freaks? Am I not giving you what you need, Celeste?" His voice drops to a low and deadly tone, "Do I not scare you enough, my Sweet? Let me fix that for you." For a moment, he releases me, only to snatch me up by the neck and shove me hard against the wood, face pinned and turned to the side. The board is filthy, I can practically *feel* the mud and dirt coating my white dress. *Say it, Celeste.* "Trick". But my heart drops at the thought. *I don't want to.*

I'm scared. But I don't want this to stop...

He steps to the side, still holding me down with one arm but releasing the pressure on my thighs and the restriction of my torso. Planting my own hands, I push against the board and swing my legs trying to loosen his grip. *If I can just get the angle right, I can kick him and make a break for it. I'll head for that fucking saloon, he wouldn't dare chase me into a place that crowded...would he?* But before I can really come to a conclusion on just how ballsy he might actually be, my train of thought is interrupted by a swift whistle and a sudden sting across my ass.

I was never whipped growing up, but I've listened to enough stories from this area to know a switch when I feel one. *Fuck.* The warmth from the impact of the small branch, which I'm assuming he collected from the ground, is spreading over my cheeks. I yelp out in pain and try to twist to see what he actually smacked me with, but his grip is unforgiving. I can barely see him at all in my peripheral vision.

He has me stuck staring at only the scattered set pieces, shadowy trees, and the dim lights on the trail in the distance while listening to the cacophony of screams around me, knowing mine will mean nothing. *I'm at his mercy...if he even has any.* I cry out again when the second lash connects. This one is lower, brushing the top of my thighs and spreading the flames farther. Tears well up in my eyes, but I am also painfully aware that my pussy is extremely wet. The stings hurt, but the way they mellow into that warmth and ache is arousing. My clit is throbbing from the abuse. *Goddamn it. This man brings out the depravity in me.* But it suddenly hits me that *that isn't the truth. He doesn't bring out the depravity...he just gives me a reprieve to explore what I already want. A space to feed my own desires without judgement. Freedom to be* me.

Another whistle sounds through the air, but this lash drawls a low groan instead of a squeal. It lands back over the original mark, bringing a fresh sting to the dulling ache. But my pussy convulses in time with the throbbing pain. So much so that I feel a pang of disappointment when I hear him toss the branch back down. However, that subsides quickly when he pulls the hem of my dress up over my full ass, exposing me to both him and the night air. His hand moves over my skin, massaging the tender flesh and soothing the ache.

"Three lashes, my Sweet. One for each of that spider's limbs I had to break for chasing my witch," he says as he continues to examine and tend to my welts.

I freeze. *The screams I heard earlier...the ones that sounded too real.* "You didn't."

The smug chuckle sends a chill down my spine. "Why do you think I snatched you off the path as early as I did? No need to leave a whole trail of mangled bodies in your wake."

If he attacked someone, it had to have been reported by now. They will be looking for him. He has to know he doesn't have long. "Why are you doing this?" I didn't use as many words and I whispered them into the night, but I know he understood what I was asking. *This is different and we both feel it. Why?*

He lets go and instinctually I pop up, spinning around to face him, only to be met with his blade to my throat and his mask inches from my face. I'm too nervous to even pull my dress back down, frozen, staring back into those dark orbs knowing that behind them is a pair of eyes boring into my soul and witnessing parts of me I've never shown anyone else.

"Because you're mine, Celeste, yet you're trying so hard not to be. Come what may to anyone else in the process, and no matter how long it takes for you to accept it, you are *mine*. These imposters can't bring you what you crave. They don't have the devotion required *but I do*. I will do anything to satisfy you. Every part of you. *Especially* those dark, divine pieces."

Stepping closer to me, he pushes the blade directly against my neck forcing me to step backwards into the board again. He keeps progressing forward until I collapse back on it as he pulls my legs apart and steps between them. He puts the tip of the blade into the underside of my chin, forcing my head up, back, and still. I hear the distinct sound of velcro being pulled.

Then I feel him crouch down, keeping his arm fully extended and the knife in place, as his breath washes over my pussy again. *Oh God, yes please.* I want it. I *crave* it. *Please make me cum on that tongue again while at knifepoint.*

As if reading my mind, his tongue drags along my slit, tasting me. He groans, making my pussy spasm right in front of his eyes. His tongue enters me, lapping before curling up and lavishing my walls. Meanwhile his lip latches over my clit as he sucks in, pulling a deep scream of pleasure from me. It echos off the trees, but he's right. It just blends into all the other cries in the night.

Instinctually, I try to look down, but the sharp point digging into the underside of my chin stops me. *Even when he's eating me, I'm at his mercy.* The thought sends a chill down my spine and only adds to the stimulation of my clit. My nipples are so hard it hurts. I can feel my pussy pulsing around his tongue. My climax is building quickly and I'm panting for it. I want another white-out, mind-blowing orgasm. *I don't care if it's caused by a stalker anymore or not. I need this sweet release.*

Not the kind that comes just from physical stimulation, but the deep soul-shattering orgasms that only arise from playing in all your deepest, darkest desires. The ones that leave you satisfied, overwhelmed, and questioning your entire life after.

But just as I feel myself starting to clench up, he stops. Pulls his warm, wet lips from my vulva and leaves me shaking and exposed to the cold. I want to look down and demand he keep going, but the knife still has me hostage so I just scream in frustration, my nails clawing against the board.

He chuckles, clicking his tongue at me. "So impatient, my Sweet." *He's fucking edging me.*

"They're coming for you, you know. If you *really* hurt that guy, they are going to have security all over this place. You don't have long, so if you're actually going to do anything, you better fucking get to it." I snap out.

Next thing I know, he's standing between my legs and jerking me into a sitting position, pressing my chest into his torso and forcing me to look up at the mask, now missing the netting in the mouth, exposing that smug smile. The scent of him is intoxicating, the desire to literally lick him washing over me like a tsunami.

I can feel a slight tremble in his hold as he speaks, "I have enough time to give you the devotion you deserve, my Sweet. To sacrifice for you and your pleasure."

He steps back, tossing the knife in the air, letting it spin again...but this time he snatches it by the blade. I gasp, instinctually reaching for him but he raises his other hand to stop me. The soulless black orbs of the mask are boring into mine. I can feel the intensity of his stare even though I can't see his real eyes, as he grips the blade tighter. Slowly, his free hand reaches farther out, caressing my face. The scent of his leather glove mixing with the aroma of his sweat has my mouth watering.

His thumb runs gently over my cheek as he brings the knife up between us. I can see where the blade has sliced through the glove and into his flesh...his blood is beginning to run out of the cut in the leather and trail down the fabric until it drips onto his arm. A path of red is streaking down his skin. Blood. *His blood.*

My gaze cuts back to the mask, searching fruitlessly for answers in those empty eyes. But I *feel* them. In the way he's touching me, the display he's making of himself - he's offering a sacrifice to me...for me. He's making a pledge.

Slowly, he lowers the knife between my legs, still gripping it by the blade. He runs the handle up and down my slick pussy lips, lubricating it. A small hiss escapes him as he begins to press it into me, forcing me to stretch around the handle. I gasp and he strokes my face again, soothing me. I know the pressure he's having to apply to push the knife inside of me must be causing it to slice deeper into him, but he doesn't hesitate. In moments, he is sliding the knife in and out of me, fucking me with it. The handle is filling me, the texture of the grip pleasantly stimulating. I can feel his hot blood running down his fist and dripping onto me, mixing with my juices. Loud moans are tumbling from me rapidly, my chest heaving, as my orgasm builds yet again.

"Ohhhh, God yes," I groan out.

He hisses, pausing his motions. In a blink of an eye, his other hand snatches my necklace, twists it around his fist, and jerks hard, ripping it from my neck. I drop my jaw in shock, only for him to violently shove the cross and chain into my mouth. I cough, trying desperately not to swallow and choke as he clasps his hand over my lips, holding the necklace inside. The chain remains wound around his fingers but the intrusion of the large cross in my mouth still feels like a choking hazard.

"Don't bring God into this, my Sweet. This is our sacred rite. I'm binding us together. Through sacrifice, through pain, and through pleasure. Fuck wherever our souls end up, right *here*, right *now*..." His words waiver, even with the voice changer he sounds so desperate and...vulnerable. "Our souls belong to one another. He has no place here with you and me. We are each other's heaven...and hell."

He slowly draws the chain from my mouth as he pulls his hand away. It tickles against my lips until the cross pops out from between them. It dangles in the air for a moment, dripping my saliva. We both stare at it until he tosses the broken necklace aside into the dirt. His hand flies back to my hair, knotting in it and making me moan as he starts thrusting the knife again.

"Cum for me, Celeste," he growls, letting it rumble and practically vibrate through my body. Then his hand runs from my hair, down my neck, and to my chest, ripping the dress cups back to expose my bare breasts to the air. The cold licking at my hard nipples as he works my walls around the textured handle has me shaking for him. His other hand massages my breasts, occasionally pinching at the nipples to make me squeal.

I toss my head backward and fall onto my elbows, back arching, chest heaving while I offer myself to him. *No more questions. No more playing pretend. I* want *this. And I don't give a damn what anyone else would think. I'm going to fucking* savor *it.* I look up at him, biting my lip in pleasure and spreading my legs wider to show him that I'm surrendering to this twisted darkness. *I'm all in.*

He whispers, "My Sweet," into the night, and I explode. The spasms that course through my body are profane, I am certain. Screaming in pleasure as I writhe for him, my mind is overwhelmed and I can't even form a coherent thought. The sensations are so intense that I didn't notice when he first pulled the knife from me and laid it aside so he could run his hands over me as I came. *Both hands.*

My dress is streaked with his fresh blood now. The warmth of it soaking through the fabric and to my skin. My pale flesh shows the red stains well, even in the night. I must look like one of the beaten angels from the wars depicted on his chest at this point. As my breathing starts to regulate and I come down from my orgasm, he picks the knife back up.

"Are you ready, Witch?"

Fear surges through my system. *Holy shit, is he actually going to kill me this time?* My voice trembles when I speak, "...for what exactly?"

"Our binding. A blood pact."

A chill runs through me, but not from fear. I stare at that demon pumpkin face and I have no doubts I'm going to do this. *It's fucking crazy. I don't even know who this man is. But he sees and understands parts of me I was too scared to even acknowledge...how could I say no? He adored me before I was willing to acknowledge who I was.*

I nod, but he takes my face in both his hands, one sticky and wet while the other is smooth against my cheek. "I need to hear you say it, Celeste."

No timidity remains in me now. Gazing into those dark orbs, searching for the eyes hidden behind them, I declare it with confidence, "I want to bind myself to you. I am yours, and you are mine."

I believe there are forces in this world that we can't explain and I have never tried to. I leave that to others to figure out, but it feels as if we are tapping into something beyond ourselves and our control. Probably messing with things we don't understand and shouldn't, but I don't care at this moment. *If this is actually* real, *then even better.* Because I mean it. *I want to be bound to this man.*

My pumpkin prince takes the knife and runs it slowly down the gap between my breasts, applying just enough pressure to split the skin and let my blood bubble to the surface. It stings, but I don't look away from him. I hear him unfastening his belt and zipper. *Fuck.* The lure to examine what he has for me is tempting, but the power of the moment feels balanced on this intense stare we are sharing. So instead of looking, I wait to feel him.

He doesn't make me wait long. In a moment, the bulbous head of his cock is running along my slick folds, coating itself in my juices and his blood. "Please..." the beg slips from my lips before I realize it. He answers with a push, invading my tight pussy and stretching me around him.

We both groan in pleasure as he works his length into me. He's thick, long, and throbbing. *Holy shit.* Instinctually, I tighten my walls, squeezing his cock inside me. He hisses, like his control is barely contained and shoves deeper, another inch filling me.

When he's buried to the hilt in my pussy, he lays his bleeding hand on my chest, flat over my cut, letting our blood mix. He pulls out slowly, teasing us both until just his head remains inside me.

"Mine," he growls, thrusting savagely, making me cry out. He presses his hand harder against my chest as he pumps in and out of me fast and hard. His pace is frantic...almost desperate. *He feels it too. This isn't just physical gratification. The stakes are too high. This is for our sanity...our souls.* He is sliding in and out of me smoothly with all the lubrication, but my walls are clinging to his girth and my jaw falls slack from the pleasure. *I'm going to cum again.*

Leaning forward over me, he places his other hand on the back of my head and brings it to his. My forehead is touching the mask's and I can hear every breath and gasp he takes behind it. *Oh shit...yes.* He is driving me wild. I grind against him, fucking back and losing myself in the lust just as much as he is until I groan in pleasure as my orgasm washes over me. Again, I shake in his grasp as I ride out the tingles and the spasms on his cock. I'm clamping down on it as he continues to fuck me through it, not slowed by my contractions. He extends it, leaving me breathless and panting as he pulls out.

But I don't get to catch my breath, suddenly I'm being snatched from the table and tossed onto the ground. More dirt and mud now added to the stains on my dress. A hand is in my hair pulling me onto my knees so I'm face to face with his cock, coated and glistening with my juices. I was right, he's a good nine inches long and thick. *No wonder I was stretching so much even after an orgasm. Holy shit.*

Suddenly I feel the cold steel of a blade against the back of my neck, right under the edge of my hair. He doesn't say a word. *He doesn't have to.* The pressure of the blade forces me forward, making me open my mouth and take his cock into it. My sweetness mixed with a hint of a metallic tang coats my tongue. My stalker groans and pushes more of himself between my lips. I place my hands on either side of his hips and dig my nails into his jeans as I run my tongue along the underside of his cock, tracing the throbbing vein there, making his hand in my hair tighten. *Good.*

I suck hard, hollowing out my cheeks. But when I try to bob my head to properly blow him, I become painfully aware of the fact that the knife isn't moving with me. It's still, keeping me in place. *If I try to retreat from his cock, it's going to cost me. Shit.*

My fucked pussy spasms at the thought, pushing a little more of my cum onto my thighs. Another inch is pushed into my mouth, forcing me to relax my throat to try to keep from gagging, but it doesn't keep my eyes from watering. I look up at him through my eyelashes, batting them so the tears run over and streak down my face. He groans, increasing the pressure of the blade against my neck and instinctually forces more of himself in my mouth.

Fuck he's big and it's throbbing. The pulse of his cock in my mouth is erotic, but it is taking all I have not to gag and cough as his member works its way into my throat. Tears are rolling freely now. Every cell in me is screaming for me to pull back and to take a deep breath, but I can't because of that fucking knife.

I gulp around him, the swallow making my throat tighten around his head and he lets out a deep growl of, "Fuck, Celeste," as he starts to throb forcefully. I can feel hot, thick shots of cum spilling directly down my throat. That distinct salty tang filling my mouth seems to make a fucking demon take hold of me and I suck harder until his knees buckle. Satisfaction floods me. *I can bring you to your knees too, Pumpkin Face.*

He pulls himself from my mouth before I can make him fully collapse, saliva trailing from my lip to the head of his cock. Quickly, he puts himself away and runs his thumb over my bottom lip wiping away the residue. The moment is sweet, tender even...and the brat in me revolts.

"Code red!" I scream at the top of my lungs, "Help!"

His hand instinctually snatches up my chin and squeezes my jaw open to try to stop me. But he must clock the mischievous glint in my eye, because he chuckles. "No one's going to be able to help you get the taste of me out of your fucking throat, my Sweet."

He releases me and walks backwards before blowing me a kiss and disappearing into the trees. *Goddamn. What did I just do?* But the answer comes to me without missing a beat. *You just bound yourself to a psycho...and you don't regret it a bit.*

I manage to push myself into a standing position while I yell out, "Code red!" again and start to work my way towards the path. But I only get halfway back to the lights and the symphony of power tools before I see another woman working her way through the trees towards me.

Savannah panicked when she saw me emerge from the woods, muddy and blood-covered, leaning on the cannibal hillbilly actress who found and helped me out of the haunt. She had been mere minutes from going to one of the trail managers to report me missing, assuming I must have run and gotten lost in the dark without a light from the "pumpkin prick" as she took to calling him.

We were there for almost an hour with me answering questions about what happened with management and security. My story was simple. The pitch black was really good this year and I actually got a little scared so I freaked and ran. I bumped into some bloody props in the process, messing up my dress. But unfortunately, I fled too far off into the woods and got turned around in the dark. Then I fell and got scuffed up. That's when I started calling for help and the actress found me. I kept reassuring them that I was fine and no one did anything wrong, but I knew what really worried them, even though they certainly weren't admitting to it, was that no one in their cast fit the description that Savannah had given them of my tormentor. They thought they had an imposter among them assaulting guests and injuring actors. Instead they just had a guest star who wanted to turn their set into my personal nightmare.

I came out of those woods changed, twisted, broken, and beautiful. *I was right. The Celeste that went into those trees with him is not the one that came back out.* The taste of him lingers in the back of my throat just as much as the thought of his blood bond lingers in my mind. Something dark and desperate transpired in those woods tonight...for us both. I don't know what it really means for the future, besides the fact that I'm certain I'll never be lonely again. I could feel it. That man is never going to leave me alone for as long as we are both breathing. Being tied in such a way to a psycho stalker is probably not healthy, but I can't help but smile anyway as I watch the night blur outside the window of Savannah's car.

Damian

I'll admit, Friday was intense. For most women I probably went way too far...but not for Celeste. *That's why we are perfect together.* We both understood that...*need.* Sure it was dark and depraved, but it was also sacred. What transpired between us was...spiritual. *And not in the fucked up twisted way I had been raised to see religion. What we did...transcends God.* Whether heaven, hell, or God himself is real or not, nothing can take what we share from Celeste and I now. *Even if I'm cast into a pit of fire, I will always have her and our love as a comfort from the torment.*

Perhaps letting myself stew for over a week before I came to her wasn't the wisest idea though. I was frenzied with anger, frustration, and *fear.* After she was in my presence and melting beneath my touch again, I knew it was okay. We could work through whatever doubts she may have. *But I can't deny that I was close to cracking beforehand. If she'd rejected me in those woods, she would've ended up in my truck and we'd be halfway across the country, holed up somewhere, no matter what I had promised myself before.* Suddenly, the "almost lost my cool there" clip from the fucking Grinch movie pops into my head.

Damn, she is driving me insane.

But I want to make it up to Celeste. Tonight is our lunar anniversary. The twelfth first quarter moon since the evening we met. I have so much planned for her and I want it all to go perfectly.

Tonight is the start of the rest of our lives.

I've stayed away all week while I was making preparations for this evening. *Watched the cameras in her house like an addict and ate my weight in caramels, but stayed away.* Well, other than class on Tuesday, but she wasn't there this time. Instead, we had to stare at Professor Beck as he droned on. Celeste is definitely more engaging as a lab instructor. *Makes sense, Chemistry is just modern witchcraft.* When I checked on her, she was at home with Osiris. I don't know whether she was *avoiding* Damian or simply *too* in her head about her stalker to come to class...*but I'm going to fix both of those tonight.* She required time to process our pact and I needed to concentrate on my plans. *Not to mention, let my hand heal.* So while it was difficult, a week apart was necessary. *But it was easier this time than it ever has been before.*

Not because I didn't miss her, or the idea of losing her is any less scary, but because I trust *that I won't after that night.* No matter how long we are away from each other, she *will* be back in my arms again. *She meant that vow. We both felt it. At this point, she's my wife as far as I'm concerned.*

The chime of Juke's door catches my attention. Celeste is standing halfway out of it, waving bye to someone inside. *Even in a simple white t-shirt and jeans, she looks great.* I let her get a few steps into the parking lot before I called to her. "Hey you!"

She practically jumps out of her skin, whipping around towards my voice. The alarm on her face melts into relief once she recognizes me, only to be quickly replaced by suspicion. "Damian?"

"Yeah, sorry, I didn't mean to startle you." I'm leaning back on the hood of my truck, arms crossed, letting her approach me as she's comfortable. *I might be busting at the seams to kiss her again, but tonight is about her. We need to take this slow, if it has a chance of going well.*

She peeks around me, glancing nervously into the dark as if she's checking for someone else. *Cute.* "Umm, hi. What are you doing here?" She tosses a thumb back towards the bar. "You know we closed like twenty minutes ago, right? Can't really get you a drink at this point."

I smirk, "What if a drink isn't the way I'd like to unwind tonight?" I lift up one hand, flashing her the joint in it.

She bites her lip. "Damian...look I don't want to be rude but -"

"Hey, no pressure. I only wanted to swing by and offer you a night out as friends. I was rude the other week and I feel terrible about it. I'd really like to make it up to you. I swear it's not a date, just a joint between friends at a spooky atmospheric hang out."

She looks up at me, those emeralds glowing in the moonlight that's washing over her hair and sweet, pale face. Her piercings sparkle even in the night. The black-painted skin of her full lips is caught between her teeth as she debates my offer. *Damn, she's stunning.*

She sneaks another glance into the dark before she replies, "Okay...*one blunt*...but then I have to head home."

"Of course." I walk around the truck and open the passenger door for her. *I'll be the one taking you there though.*

The conversation on the way to our surprise destination was pleasant but shallow. She's nervous. *Poor thing.* Celeste is probably worried that her stalker will be pissed she's out with me...especially after that pact. *Granted, I might be if it was anyone other than me.*

But I know that she wouldn't be so tempted to go with just anyone else. It's because it is *me* that she's unable to resist. Her mind may not have pieced it together but her body knows

Damian and her pumpkin nightmare are one and the same. Our scents, pheromones, body language, etc; there are so many subtle signs that her sympathetic nervous system is interpreting. *Eventually her prefrontal cortex will catch up.*

She lets out a small, amazed gasp as we pull into the graveyard just outside of town. "Here we are. Figured this is the kind of place we can hang out and smoke and the neighbors won't complain." I look over at her and smirk.

She's jumping out of the truck before I even have a chance to get around the cab. "Damian! This is such a cool idea!" Celeste is already trudging up to the first row of headstones, bent forward to inspect the engravings closely in the dark, putting her big, round, beautiful behind up in the air.

Focus.

I clear my throat as I walk up next to her, holding out a miniature flashlight, "Thought this might be helpful." She squeals and snatches it from me excitedly. For a few minutes, I simply enjoy the view of her bounding along the rows, reading all the headstones. She's *giddy. That's my spooky girl.* I cup my hand around the end of the blunt as I light it, inhaling just enough for it to take. I want to save as much of it as I can for her...*she's going to need it tonight.*

"Celeste?" I hold the burning blunt towards her and she skips over to retrieve it.

She inhales deeply, holding the hit in for a count of five before exhaling the smoke into the night, a slight cough following it. "You know, I wouldn't have pegged you for a *marijuana* user," she whispers conspiratorially before laughing. *There it is. My favorite sound in the world...other than her screams in orgasm.*

"Oh? Why's that? Does the lack of shaggy hair and psychedelic attire help me slip past your nineteen-seventies based cliches?"

She chuckles, trying to hold in her second hit as she passes the blunt back to me. I take a small one, not wanting to make it obvious that this isn't really for us both. But I'm so focused on how big of a breath I'm taking that I don't pay attention to the speed and I end up hacking up a lung in response. I shove the blunt back at her as I double over, clearing out my lungs.

Celeste is sporting a smug, naughty grin as she carefully collects it from me, "No smartass. *That's why.*" She giggles and lifts it to her lips again as she starts to walk down a new row of headstones.

My voice is raspy as I stand upright to follow her, "It's just been awhile, I'm not a teenager anymore. I mean when's the last time you smoked?"

"Last Halloween," she answers immediately without a thought. The scent of weed and her perfume is leaving an intoxicating trail for me to follow through the graveyard, taking me back to that very same night. *The one that set us both on a path to end up right here, right now, together.*

"Oh, like to party on Halloween, huh? Considering your house I could've guessed that."

Her laugh echoes across the field of graves, bringing a touch of life to the place. "Oh no, I love Halloween, and even a party on occasion, but normally *Halloween parties* are a no for me. However, it was a costume one and my best friends were going so I brought the weed so I could attend *and* relax."

I flash her my wicked grin, "Costume party? What did you go as?"

Taking one more hit before she passes the blunt back to me, she exhales as she answers. "A witch." I stop where I am, letting her get a little space between us.

Celeste bends down, brushing her hair behind her ear as she uses the flashlight to read another engraving. I reply, "A witch? Hmmm, what are you going as this year?"

She answers me absentmindedly, "A witch again."

"Now, Celeste, aren't you supposed to go as something you aren't for Halloween?"

She bolts up, hands on her chest in mock offense, "Oh, you think I'm a witch? Harumph," she spins on her heels and starts to walk away from me.

"Who else does blood pacts in the woods?"

I don't know what kind of reaction I was expecting from her exactly - rage, tears, panic, maybe even catatonia, but I certainly wasn't expecting for her to just stop midstep and turn to me with a blank look on her face.

"What?" She says it calmly.

The silence that settles into the air is heavy, *even for a graveyard.*

"I said, who else does blood pacts in the woods?"

She doesn't miss a beat. "So you're pumpkin face? You, Damian LaCroix, are my stalker," she lifts one hand in a gentle wave. "Just so we are clear, that's what you're saying." She stares at me expectantly.

There's no point in pretending to be ashamed. *I did it and I'd do it again.* "Yes, Celeste, I am." I take one gentle step towards her, testing her reaction.

She blinks twice before she doubles over laughing maniacally and starts meandering through the headstones again. *Okay...that doesn't seem good.*

"Of - fucking - course you are! That makes perfect sense. Honestly, I should've known. Why wouldn't the only other guy I've actually liked in my adult life turn out to be the only other psycho I've known in my life!"

Ouch. "I know this -"

She whips back around, storming up the row at me. Finally finding that rage I was expecting, "You. Know.

Nothing. Don't you fucking dare try to relate to me when you've been not only stalking me *for a year* but then decided to *date* me as well? What the fuck? Do you know how much true crime I watch? And that's even new to me."

"In all fairness to me, I wasn't planning to date you, well, not like *this* originally...it just kinda happened when I couldn't stay away from you and we hit it off -" I stop when I see the way her eyes are raging at me. *Shit, this is going to be worse than I thought.*

"Why wouldn't you just approach me and ask me out? Clearly, we have chemistry and attraction. We always have. Everything has been so easy since we started dating...even at that party, we both *apparently* felt that connection. So why all of this bullshit? Unless you're pretending to be someone you aren't. Is that it? Of course it is!" She's in my face, spewing her words.

There's the trust issues. *You can't really say shit. You didn't exactly help relieve them by living a double life with her.* Fuck. *Just tell her the truth.*

"You stalk me for months so you can figure out what kind of man I want and then you what? Swing right in and act like him until I fall so you have me in a place I'll compromise myself? Just a lovesick girl who will do whatever you want!" She lets out a guttural scream of frustration as she storms away from me again. "How could I be so stupid?!"

Her yells are echoing across the field. If I was more superstitious I'd be afraid she would wake the dead. "I didn't co-" but she interrupts me again.

"Men like you, *like Issac*, I don't fucking understand you. Why are you all so obsessed with selecting some random girl and manipulating her by being whoever you have to until she loves you enough to let you break her. Why don't you just go get women who are already who you want? Does the power give you some kind of sick satisfaction? It's pathetic!"

I don't know what comes over me, I've never knelt to anyone in my life. *But I'm desperate. I'm shameless for Celeste.* When she turns around to face me this time, I'm on my knees, in the dirt, looking up at her. "Please, listen to me. Just for a minute. If you don't feel different after...we will deal with that. But please...let me try to explain."

Her eyes soften slightly though she remains where she is, arms crossed and standoffish. But I take her silence as permission to continue.

"I didn't simply approach you and ask you out because I didn't deserve you, Celeste. I couldn't just walk up to the gates of Heaven and demand entry with the man I was...*the man I am.* But I couldn't stay away either. Once I saw you, there was no hope for me. You were...*are*...my chance at peace and happiness in this life."

She's analyzing every twitch of my face, eyes as sharp as a hawk's. "What do you mean by the man you are?"

I breathe deep, licking my lip as I prepare for this. "I've done some terrible shit in my life."

"Like?"

Damn it, I knew this was coming, but it's still harder to admit than I expected. My stomach is in such tight knots that I don't even think I'm physically capable of throwing up, no matter how nauseous I am. I meet her gaze and pray to *her* that the truth works.

"I've hurt people, Celeste. A lot of people. My family has a long history of criminal activity. We have our hands in a variety of...enterprises along the lower East Coast. I didn't get involved until I was a teenager, but I found a place as an enforcer pretty easily and caught up quickly."

She takes a few cautious steps my way, before she sinks down and sits on her butt with her legs crisscrossed on top of the grave in front of me. "You got involved as a teenager?"

I look off into the dark as I head into the memories I try desperately to avoid...but if I want Celeste to accept every part of me then she deserves to hear it all. "Yeah, they found out about me late. My mother was the only daughter in her generation. Apparently the LaCroix leave their girls out of the family business. But she *knew* what they did of course. She threw herself into the church, believing she could pray away the sins of the family. I've heard since, that she wasn't so...*zealous*...back then. Just devout. Apparently she snapped after my father left her, pregnant and alone. So fast she didn't even have time to file a name change. No one was willing to tell me much, *not even who he was*." I scoff.

"But they were married and then he just up and left - disappeared. Next thing the family knew, my mother had taken off herself and no one could find her. What she did was jump on a random bus, with what cash she could get away with, and relocate to a city halfway across the country, where she started working at a church in exchange for a studio apartment. She told them she was widowed. She had a marriage license, that she promptly burned after, to prove I wasn't a bastard so they accepted her. Honestly, I don't know why they didn't ask for his death certificate, maybe they assumed she was actually fleeing an abusive husband, I don't know. But they certainly cared if she was actually fucking married since she was pregnant. Heaven forbid they might help a whore and her bastard child." I spit into the dirt beside me. The bile building up in my throat is too much to keep inside. I *hated* those hypocrites.

I still can't look at Celeste, desperate to get it all out before I choke up and shove it down into the pit again. "My mother went crazy. The religion seeped in and warped her trauma and grief. She became convinced my father was a demon who had found his way to her because of her family's sins. He married her simply to impregnate her with his devil spawn and then leave her alone to raise it within the LaCroix family so that it could flourish in the sin they spread. That's why she named me Damian. You'd think a demon baby would've been cause enough for an abortion but apparently that is such a horrible sin there isn't even an exception for devil spawn, so she had to have me either way. Before I arrived, she decided that I was her penance for being a LaCroix and her calling was to try to *save* me. Though she spent my entire childhood telling me it was an impossible task. She was Sisyphus and my soul her stone. "

Her voice flashes through my head, "Names have meaning. They set the course of someone's life. You were born damned, boy, no need pretending you will ever be more than the demon you were bred to be." My fists dig into the soft, moist soil beneath me as I ground myself.

The warmth of her hands surprise me as Celeste lays her own over mine, pulling me from the pain battering around in my head. "Please," she whispers, "keep going. You are safe here."

Am I? I know she won't physically hurt me and that my mother isn't actually going to come out of the dark and beat me again. But Celeste could shatter me in ways that my mother never managed to do to my bones.

"I grew up in the shadow of an extremist church where they tried to teach me to hate everyone and everything that wasn't *holy* like them. But my mother made it clear I was a damned sinner myself so why should I hate those who are like me? Their messages never took. And by the time I was old enough to really read their book, usually while I was laid up in bed healing from whatever *penance* my mother thought I owed God, I learned they were all hypocrites. I rebelled, which only led to harsher beatings, but I didn't care. I refused to be complicit. When I was sixteen, I had a job and was already putting money away to leave when Kage found me."

"Kage?" Celeste asks quietly into the night.

I nod. "My cousin. He was a couple years older than me. Just old enough to remember his aunt that had disappeared and all the rumors that abounded about her child. He was wanting to make a play within the family. He was *unsatisfied* with the hierarchy. But no one else was willing to act against blood like that...so he sought out the only member who had a right to the family name just like he did who wouldn't have ties to all the people who shared it"

I pause, breathing in the night air, trying to cool my body. It feels like a sweat could break out across it at any moment. Celeste reaches up and strokes my cheek, finally pulling my attention to her beautiful face. She's looking at me with...*grace* - with an acceptance, forgiveness...*dare I say it? With love.*

My eyes lock on her stunning emeralds as I continue, "By the time I was nineteen we had eliminated a lot of my family. Kage was like a brother to me. He had pulled me from hell and given me freedom and *purpose*. He told me everything he could about my real history, not the warped and twisted tale my mother had fed me my entire life. He gave me power and respect. So what if I had to maim or kill to get it? I wasn't about to let it go. It was easy to transition into killing criminals when I had been beaten to the brink of death repeatedly for what I *might* become. They chose this life. That was on them. By the time Kage started aiming me towards people who weren't as *guilty*, I was too far gone to care. I had a job, I did it, and I moved on to the next one. Kage called me his enforcer, but most of the time I was more of an executioner."

The moisture that is collecting in her eyes is reflecting the moonlight back at me. "I was with Kage for basically a decade before I got out. Somewhere along the way, the rage from my childhood started to burn out. Never gone, but under control enough that I could see things clearer. Kage was headed down paths I didn't *want* to follow. It was complicated, but I managed to walk away and start life again. I picked a small town...Ammerton, learned a blue collar skill, and had settled down, expecting to spend the rest of my life alone until I died and God finally got to take his vengeance out on me like Mother always said. I lived like that for nine years, until I ended up at this Halloween party with some witch," I wink at her, making her snort and roll her eyes, "who absolutely turned my life upside down."

"Damian," Celeste whispers, "it was one kiss."

"No. You were my heaven personified. My one chance at happiness and peace before I burn in hell. How could I let that go? I *knew* I was being crazy and unhinged...but knowing didn't stop me. I needed you, Celeste...I still do. I will until the day I die. Every moment I have watched you, I have fallen deeper and deeper in love with you."

Her eyes widened at the word *love*. I reach out and cup her face in both my hands, ignoring the dirt I'm marring it with. "I love every part of you, Celeste, even the darkness you were afraid of. I *understand* it. We are uniquely matched to see, accept, and *love* a darkness in each other that most people would run from."

She's staring at me, hanging on every word. *This moment is integral, don't fuck this up, Damian.* "I'm not Issac. I didn't watch you to become something you want so I could change you. I watched you to survive until I could be a semblance of what's worthy enough for the magnificent creature you are, *just* as you are. I would never change you, Celeste."

"But-"

"Even if you never forgive me, I can't regret what I did because you deserve to love every part of *yourself*, Celeste. To hell with what anyone else has ever told you about what's 'acceptable', 'ladylike', 'proper', or any of their other pathetic mortal standards. You are a Goddess. You *fucking transcend* them."

Her full lips are quivering, doubt and belief roiling in her eyes like waves in a storm, as she listens to me.

"And even if it cost me your acceptance of us, it was worth it to see you step into yourself. I know you've felt it. I've watched you. With every game we play, you embrace more and more of that darkness that you've tried to hide away."

Suddenly, I'm toppling backwards as her body collides with mine. She's wrapped herself around me and is crushing her lips against my own, kissing me passionately. I relax back against the earth, gently holding her as I let her take control.

Her lips are silky, warm, and still taste of the sweet familiar flavor. Our kiss is tender, a little frantic in need, but genuinely soft. She breaks it, but doesn't pull away. The words are merely breathed against my lips, but I hear them loud and clear.

"I love you, Damian."

Celeste

I said it. I can't believe that Damian just confessed to me that he is my fucking stalker and that conversation somehow progressed to me saying I love you! *But I guess I'm just as fucking insane as he is...because I meant it.*

I do love him. Especially, now that I know he isn't just the amazing guy who treats me well and makes me feel seen and heard, but he is also my favorite twisted nightmare who adores every fucked up part of me and brings me pleasures I've never had before. It's no wonder I couldn't resist him on either side of our lives.

Though I am irritated that he let me stress myself out for weeks over having feelings for one man and lusting another. He owes me big time for all of that angst. Someday, I'll tell him how he inadvertently pushed me to overthink us into a breakup and we can both laugh about it, but tonight I just want to focus on us and our bond.

I made that pact in the woods with my stalker...but deep down I think a part of me knew. I've only felt that comfortable and safe with two men since Issac, one of which wore a mask. I *probably* should've logically pieced that shit together, but I think my soul already had. *Bitch just decided to keep it to herself.*

Damian turns the truck into my driveway, the sound of the gravel pulling me from my thoughts. I glance over at him, my eyes falling on the witch pin up tattoo of me, on his forearm, that he exposed when he rolled up his sleeves as we left the graveyard. *I can't believe I never noticed that he was* always *wearing long sleeves. Geez, I should* not *become a detective.*

Tonight is the first quarter moon, the twelfth since we met, and apparently he has plans for us until morning. He told me he has a very special gift this time. A big part of me is hoping that it is something that will end up in another mind-blowing orgasm. *Please.*

But as long as we are spending the night together, I'll be satisfied. After everything that transpired in that graveyard...everything we said and shared...I couldn't bear to be away from him right now. *We are meant to be together, and tonight, I say that* very *literally.*

After he parks the truck, Damian comes around to open the door for me, holding his hand out and helping me down. He looks good, sporting boots, dark jeans, and a black shirt. Simple, but perfect to highlight his good looks. His hair is swept to the side, his fiery eyes alight with mischief, and his sly grin already in place. *He's pleased with how the night's going.*

"You look like you are up to something...am I in trouble?" I ask suspiciously.

He laughs, "Someone is," and winks at me before grabbing my hand and leading me towards the cornfield.

Quickly I glance back at the house, letting my feet drag to slow us down, "Wait, we aren't going inside?" *What the hell?*

"Nope," even though he's looking away from me, I know he has that smug smirk on his face. I can *hear* it.

He continues to pull me into the field until I relent and follow him in. The stalks are planted densely, smacking us as we worm our way between them, trying to disturb as few as possible. I'm clumsily passing through the rows to keep up with Damian. Meanwhile, he's moving through them like it's nothing, even though he's at least twice my size. *How much time has he spent out here?* Wait. *Was he actually watching me from the corn all those nights I thought he might be?* It hits me that Damian and I have *a lot* to talk about.

...I kinda hope he was. The idea that he was as obsessed with me as I thought makes my panties wet. *It's dumb,* of course *he was obsessed - he was stalking you...but* how *obsessed? Goddamn it, Celeste, stop it. You're acting like a fucking high schooler.*

The corn is tall. It's even over Damian's head and would be very disorienting if it wasn't for the lone scarecrow in the field and the fact that I know where it is positioned in relation to the road and my house. He seems to be leading us directly towards it. *I wonder if that's where he left the gift so he wouldn't lose it in the sea of corn...but why not leave it at the house? He's* clearly *comfortable going in and out whether I'm there or not.*

It feels a little silly, but it's sweet. He's putting in effort and being creative to be romantic. I am *not* going to complain about that. A man who cares enough to show that I'm worth attention and energy is all I've ever wanted. Now I have it...and I couldn't be happier - no matter how crazy the path to get it might've been.

As we break through the perimeter of the corn, into the small clearing with the scarecrow, I immediately start looking for my familiar black boxes or orange bows. But there isn't much here, other than some stair steps, a small tool bag, and the scarecrow himself...with a bow tied around his stomach. *What?*

I have to take a few steps closer before the details become clear in the moonlight.

This is not what I assumed when I thought he was getting creative...

The scarecrow strung up before me doesn't have straw protruding from his shirt and overalls. He has hands...and feet...and a *familiar* face. Even unconscious and slumped forward under a wide brimmed hat, Issac's carefully maintained mug is unmistakable. A tremble makes its way through my body. *What did he do?* I take another step, confirming the rise and fall of Issac's chest.

"Damian...what is this?"

His voice is solemn and low as he responds, but I'm unable to tear my eyes away from the scarecrow to look at him. "A sacrifice for a goddess. I've given you tributes every first quarter moon since I met you and tonight I am offering you the suffering of the man who dared to deny your divinity and brought you pain."

The world starts to spin as I have to remind myself to breathe. *This can't be real. It's like a fever dream.*

"But only if you want it, my Sweet. You are the deity here, judgement is yours. I will let him go if you so wish."

I spin to face him. *Is he really giving me that kind of power? I mean he just told me an hour ago he used to kill people...professionally, I guess...but he'd just let him go if I said so?* Damian's standing at the edge of the clearing, hands in his pockets, watching me intently. His smoldering eyes locked on mine.

"...Did he see your face or where he is?" I ask timidly as I consider our options.

Damian shrugs. "Yeah, but you and I could always take off together. Some rich white boy bitching about what amounts to a bad hazing prank so far isn't going to exactly set the FBI after us or some shit."

I glance back at Issac. Hanging unconscious and limply from the post, he hardly looks like a threat...or a man who could've destroyed me emotionally for years. But the memories of his face twisted in rage as he spit his insults and degradations in mine are seared in my brain. The sight of him makes my entire body pull in on itself, like I don't even fit into my own skin properly when he's around. *But does that earn him the death penalty?* I know Damian thinks it does. An act against his Goddess calls for damnation...*but I'm not quite as sold on my divinity as he is yet.*

"If he's already seen you, then there's no harm in having a conversation with him before I decide, is there?"

Damian's eyes narrow slightly, but he nods in agreement before walking to the step stool and climbing it. Producing a small capsule from his shirt pocket, he snaps it under Issac's nostrils. Startling awake, the living scarecrow yells out and blows harshly through his crunched up nose. Damian retreats down the stairs and takes up the space behind me...*he naturally knows exactly the kind of support and protection I need.*

"Hello, Issac. Fancy meeting you out here. Doesn't really seem like your scene."

He fights against his restraints, causing the post to shake, but it holds. "What the fuck? The hell is this shit, Celeste! Cut me down right now, you bitch! Don't play fucking coy with me."

"Oh? Like you did when you showed up at Juke's the other week? *Unlike you,* I actually didn't know you were going to be here when I arrived." The sass in my voice is sharp...and smug. I don't know if it's him being tied up and distressed or having Damian at my back, but I'm *not* scared of Issac. There's no tremble in my hand or tears welling up in my eyes. I feel...*strong. Let him cower to me.* His grunts as he tugs on the binds are weak, he's tiring already. *Pathetic.*

Issac's hate-filled eyes cut to me. "Yeah right, bitch, like you didn't have your wanna be thug boyfriend over there come after me. What? Too weak and immature to handle me yourself?" His face turns into a lewd leer, "Or too afraid to be alone with me because you know you can't resist me, babydoll?"

His old nickname for me makes my skin crawl. I can feel Damian's body heat rolling off him as it rises with the strain of containing the rage that's clearly struggling to break free. I reach behind me and take one of his hands, stroking the back of it with my thumb, hoping to calm him a little bit.

"Issac. I'm trying to have a mature and civil conversation with you. Personally, I'd suggest you watch your mouth and ego moving forward if you want this to go peacefully." I say calmly, knowing damn well that he's incapable of it. I spent years with him, begging for simply that and he never could manage it. *But I need to be sure...*

Issac lurches his head forward and spits at me. "Shut the fuck up, Celeste. We both know you aren't going to do anything, you never have. And your overgrown pretty boy isn't either. He may be big, but faces that nice don't do well in prison. So cut me down and I'll make sure the DA doesn't go too hard on the both of you." He looks at me smugly. *Even now, he still thinks he can just decide to win.*

I tense around Damian's hand and whisper, "Knees."

He squeezes back in acknowledgement before stepping around me without hesitation and going to the tool bag.

Issac lolls his head, sarcasm dripping from his voice, "Really, dude? What are you, some kind of pussy-whipped errand boy for this trashy bitch? I promise I had it for years and there isn't anything there worth catching charges ov-" his insult devolves into a choked out, gurgling of a yell as he tries to scream and not vomit simultaneously.

Damian had extracted a hammer from his bag and brought it crashing, with a full-force swing, into his knee-cap. The screams of pain drowned out the sound of shattering bone, but I have no doubt that only shards remain. His eyes are wild - filled with panic, pain, and fear when he finally looks back at me. *Good.*

"You stupid bitch. Celeste, I swear to God, if you don't cut me down and take me to a hospital right now, you will live the rest of your life in prison." Seething through those perfect teeth, his breath fogs in the cool night air. His cheeks, ruddy from the pain, make him look as if he's painted to be the very scarecrow he's strung up as.

Damian swings again, shattering the other kneecap and renewing Issac's symphony of shrieks and cries. I would be worried someone might hear, but there's no one else for almost two miles. *If no one ever heard my screams, they certainly aren't going to hear his.*

I stare at him coldly. "Why did you come looking for me, Issac? No more pretending. No more manipulation. We both *know* you hunted me down and you've been following me. I want to know *why.*"

He tries to sound tough, but he struggles through the tears of pain and streams of snot marring his face. "Oh please, don't be so fucking full of yourself, bitch. I didn't want anything from you and I didn't follow you. We ran into each other at a fucking bar one night and then you fabricate this whole thing about me *following* you? You're fucking crazy. But I guess everyone knows that from the way you decided to ruin yourself with the tattoos and trashy hair. Fucking red flag for mental instability."

Lies. Gaslighting. Deflecting with insults. It's all the same. Men like Issac never change.

I lock eyes with him as I walk up to the base of the post and place my hand out towards Damian, "Knife please." He seems shocked, but doesn't argue, immediately pulling it from the sheath in the back of his waistband and placing it in my hand. The knife we've used in all our games...*the knife I started the new chapter of my life with is the same one I'll use to close the last.*

Damian climbs off the step stool and out of my way as I ascend, his hand flying to my lower back to keep me steady. *So thoughtful in every small gesture...yet society and people call him a demon, when the real one is right in front of me. It's people who lie, manipulate, play with, and break the minds and hearts of others for their own selfish reasons that are demons. Not people like Damian...like me. Not the beaten and broken who are finding their way in this dark, fucked up world filled with real demons.* And now Damian and I will find our way through it together.

I take the knife in two hands and slice down the front of his shirt and overalls, pressing hard to make sure I can cut through the thick fabrics, while not caring one bit that the tip of the blade has pierced his skin. It is ripping through him as well. I jerk quickly, slicing through the surface of his chest and stomach along with the clothes. Blood begins rapidly spilling out from either side of the blade, soaking into the fabric and gushing over the knife and my hands.

Huh. Maybe horror movies do desensitize you. Because I'm not phased at all by his blood, screams, or pain. *Or maybe this is just who I really am and I'm fully embracing it.*

I can't help it, *Scream* comes to mind. *"Don't you blame the movies. Movies don't create psychos. Movies make psychos more creative!"*

"Celeste! Fuck! Stop! Stop! Okay, I was following you! Shit! Just stop!" He pleads through the cries of pain. I look up at him, pulling the knife back as a reprieve.

"Why?"

He breathes deep, trying to find his voice despite the agony. His blood is still spilling out, staining the scarecrow outfit and dripping onto me as I stand on the steps under him. Hot and wet, the blood steams on my skin against the night air.

"Because I wanted you back. Alison *bored* me. I love your spark, Celeste, your fight. I need someone to challenge me," his eyes turn pleading. "I love you, I still do, okay? Just take me to a hospital, we can say this was from an accident. No one has to know, and then you and I can be together again! I promise. I'm sorry, I'm proud and I'm mean, but it's just because I don't know how to handle how I feel about you. But

I can fix that, okay? You forgive me for that, I forgive you for this, and we can start fresh!" He's practically feral with desperation.

I take a slow step down and then another. *There it is. A shred of the truth.* He wanted me back because of my fight. He doesn't love me of course, he never has and never will. But he got *bored* with the girl that already was his perfect little image because his power comes from subjecting a woman into being something she's not. *And the fire apparently makes it better.*

But even Issac saw something I didn't. When I doubted and lost respect for myself for staying with him and his abuse for so long, I thought I was weak and broken. But even *he* saw I was a warrior. Damian did as well. *And now I do too.*

Warrior goddesses leave no enemies standing.

I clear the last step down and look at Damian. "I'm tired of listening to him, I'm done with this conversation."

Damian's eyes light up. "Finally, my Sweet," he says as he bounds up the steps and aggressively snatches Issac's chin, squeezing his mouth open. Those irritatingly perfect teeth reflect the moonlight. Damian stares into Issac's eyes as the scarecrow attempts to mumble through his grip in vain. Even without the mask or the voice changer, I hear my Pumpkin Prince when he speaks, "You have no one to blame but yourself. She started by looking for a reason to show you mercy, again proving she is far better than you ever deserved to look at, and yet you spite her. I promise you," Damian's voice goes quiet and calm, "I have no desire to show you mercy."

With his other hand, Damian lifts the hammer and slowly slides the claw into Issac's mouth, between his teeth. Drawing out the panic and fear from him before he suddenly jerks down savagely.

The cracking of his teeth wars with the moist ripping sound of his flesh as Damian unhinges Issac's lower jaw. His eyes bulge from his head and blood gushes from the remains of his mouth. It hangs from one side now, the ligaments, muscle, and skin on the other completely torn away. Standing under them both, the gore is raining down on me, soaking my clothes and staining my skin. *But I don't care. I'll never have to hear him speak another fucking word.*

That thought makes me feel lighter, freer, and more at peace. If my peace comes at the cost of blood, then so be it. *I'm done living by anyone else's rules.*

Damian looks back down at me, a huge devilish smile on his face as he offers me a hand. Scooting over, he makes room for me to slip by and join him on the steps. Up close, I can't help but smile smugly. His teeth are broken and scattered within the chaos that was his mouth. He's alive. Gargling and spewing blood, looking at me in pure pain and fear, but alive. *Not for long though, he will bleed out any minute at this rate.*

Damian places his hand over mine and guides the blade to Issac's throat. "Are you ready, my Sweet?" he whispers. I nod in response and in a flash we have jammed the blade into one side of his neck and wrenched it across his throat, opening a gaping wound.

Issac's eyes blow wide one last time before they dull, the life seeping from them. Blood sprays, coating us both, but not like it does in my slashers. *Though that might be because he had already lost so much blood.*

Suddenly, I'm being turned and snatched off the steps, held up in the air and spun, as if we were in a fairytale and not both absolutely covered in gore. When he stills, Damian stares up at me in his arms, a look of utter amazement and devotion apparent on his face. "You are magnificent, Celeste."

I lean forward, taking his face between my hands and kiss him gingerly. Ignoring the metallic taste that's mixing with our passion. *Though I have to admit, it is the best that Issac ever tasted. Being off Damian's lips really helped the man out.* Gently setting me down, Damian brushes my hair back from my face, tucking it behind my ear for me. "The night's not over yet, my Sweet."

Celeste

We are sitting silently in the cab of his truck, cruising through the night. The sea of crops are swaying in the inky darkness as we speed by. My mind is whirling with what we just did...no regrets though. Not one bit. *Issac systematically took me apart for years and watched me suffer, why shouldn't the same happen to him? I just made sure he would never heal from it.* I believe Damian is giving me space to process the evening, but surprisingly I *don't* need it. Sure, we just killed someone together...but he was horrible. He deserved it. *He was never going to let me be.*

And deep down...*I liked it.* I don't mean in a way that I'm going to run off and become a serial killer or some shit...but giving *him* back every bit of the pain he caused me all those years was *cathartic.* And I love Damian even more for seeing the true me and what I needed, because without him I never would've allowed myself to explore those darker places.

He's right. Fuck normal or acceptable. Fuck society's or anyone else's opinions on what we did. I took my vengeance, as any slighted Goddess should. *Damian's adoration of me is going to my head so fast...and I don't care. Let him worship me because I'm done denying any part of myself.* I can't keep the smile off my face. Being fully me is clearly freeing and fulfilling...*or maybe it's just the high.*

Damian's right hand slides over the bench seat to squeeze my thigh and then come to rest there. I glance down at the dry, smeared blood staining his strong, veiny hands and my pulse quickens. I look over at him, still splattered and a mess. His eyes are locked on the road, but I can't help but admire the way his black hair is wild and tousled or how the red splashes make a tableau across his chiseled jawline. He looks dangerous...and smoking hot.

Not to mention how fucking sexy he looked as he took Issac apart. It was vicious, graphic, and merciless...everything I feared he might be when he was chasing me around like one of my horror movie killers. But to see it fully unleashed was thrilling. My panties are still soaked. *If I'm being completely honest with myself...I wanted to fuck him right there in the field and fingerpaint on each other's bodies with Issac's blood.*

I picture drawing a giant red heart over the tattoos on Damian's chest and can't suppress my giggle. *Oh yeah, I've clearly cracked too.* Oh well, I guess we will just live happily ever after in a blood soaked delulu land together.

I'm good with that.

"What's so funny, my Sweet?" he asks without looking over at me. I notice a touch of relief spread across his face. *I knew he was nervous.*

Silly man.

We made a pact. I'm not going anywhere...even if this shit didn't turn me on...yeah, it's definitely not just the high.

"Oh nothing, just admiring the view."

"A little dark to see much, isn't it?" But I can hear the jest in his tone. *He's not dense, just a smartass.*

I can be one too.

"Not the *corn*, I meant *moi*," I dramatically lift my arms and show them off, the same bloody streaks covering them as he has. "Red is definitely my color. I look incredible."

He sneaks a glance over at me with that delectably sinful smirk on his face. "Yes. You certainly do." His eyes rake over me, sending a chill down my spine before he looks back out to the road.

I should be stressing about the body strung up in a field outside my fucking house, but all I want to do is jump this man's bones. *Probably should be worried about prison too...*but Damian assured me he had it handled and I trust him.

That realization hits me like a ton of bricks and for a moment, time stops.

I trust Damian.

I never thought I would trust again. Even when I was healing and working towards dating, the goal was to find someone to be happy with and not live the rest of my life alone...but I never believed I would trust a partner again.

Yet here I am. Who knew going a little crazy in one way could help heal the crazy in another? Wild.

The truck turns sharply, suddenly pulling into a makeshift gravel lot. If Damian hadn't stopped here, I doubt I would have even noticed the break in the corn along the road. The headlights come to rest on a sign that says "Halton's Hayrides and Cornmaze". *Interesting.* They must be very small or brand new, because I've never heard of them and Ammerton isn't exactly huge. The place is abandoned, except for us. Which makes sense, as it's almost five in the morning.

This has been an insane night...and I'm still not ready for it to be over.

"And what exactly are we doing here?" I ask conspiratorially.

Damian lifts his eyebrows suggestively, "Playing a game, my Sweet." He places one hand under my chin and lifts it, so we are staring into each other's eyes. "Maybe I still have a few...urges I need to let out."

I try to fake a scared little gasp, but I can't hide the glee in my eyes. *This is going to be fun.*

"Celeste, we have just over an hour until sunrise. I'm going to give you a thirty second headstart. *Then I come for you.*" His voice is low and growly, sending chills down my spine and straight to my clit. "*If* you manage to avoid me until sunrise *or* make it out of the maze before I catch you, then you win."

"And if I don't?"

His smile grows downright feral, "*When* you don't, you are *mine*." The way he says it makes my knees weak and I'm thankful I'm sitting down. Damian sits back, resting his arm on the seat, "Now...thirty...twent-"

"Wait, what? No fair!" I yell out as I struggle with the door handle, desperately fighting to get it open, and hoping out like a panicked, clumsy prey animal.

"-nine," he stresses the word loudly as I stumble over my own feet, careening for the corn maze.

His voice is fading as I try not to trip over the gravel. "Twenty-eight...twenty-seven..." Not daring to waste time by looking back, I bound recklessly onto the path that leads into the stalks and take off full speed into the dark.

But the running is purely out of instinct, the way he looked at me triggered my fight or flight response...like he was going to eat me alive...so I ran even though this prey definitely *wants* to be caught. "Twenty-six..."

Damian

I check my reflection in the rearview mirror, making sure the mask is on straight and looks good for my Sweet. *Seven.* Popping open the door, I jump out and shove the small coil of silk rope into my pocket. *Six.*

Turning towards the exit on the left of the parking lot, I start strolling that way. *Five...Four...Three.* The gravel crunches underfoot, loud against the only other sound in the night - the brushing together of the stalks in the gentle wind. *Two.* I pause at the mouth of the path, refusing to cheat.

Celeste is mine. All of her. Every dark, beautiful, unfathomably perfect part of her - she's given me willingly now.

One. I step through the exit and head into the maze. I've been coming to Halton's all week, memorizing this labyrinth, walking it over and over. Just so I could make sure this was a game I wouldn't lose.

I knew we'd be here after Issac one way or another, but I wasn't sure *exactly* what state of mind she would be in at that point. In case she was a little more...frightened...than I hoped, I needed to make sure there was no chance she'd "win" and possibly get away from me...maybe even go to the police. Kidnapping her would've been difficult enough straight from the maze, I certainly didn't want to have to try to snatch her from somewhere else with a warrant for murder hanging over me as well. So, I spent *hours* in here memorizing the layout.

Not that I needed it.

Celeste was magnificent. Regal. Divine. She was the wrathful God I had been taught we should all fear and I loved it. I almost fell to my knees in awe of her. Honestly, I had expected Celeste to just watch me work as her avenger tonight, but her desire to join in? Shocked me. Thrilled, excited, even turned me on...but shocked me. *Her darkness was more repressed and bursting at the seams than even I realized.* Damn, every time I turn around she's showing me just how perfect she really is.

Watching her, coated in blood, as she reclaimed her power, respect, and *herself* from that prick was one of the most beautiful things I've ever witnessed in my life. The sacred rite of a Goddess taking back her place in the world and I was blessed to witness it.

Celeste is the only God I will ever worship again. I will sing her praises and do her bidding until my last breath. People think my mother was devout, but they have no idea *what devout is. I will show the world what true devotion is by her side. And anyone who stands in our way can wait their turn to greet me in hell.*

At the third intersection, I take a right. *Turn at the next left, then go around the curve into a fork, go right again.* I'm having to think through the path backwards to stay on track. I learned the maze from the entrance before I came up with the idea to start at the end. *That way she can't get out without running into me.* Sneaky, but not cheating. I said I'd come for her, but I *never* said from where. *I don't intend to lose this game.*

Just because she isn't going to run away from me, doesn't mean I want to lose out on what I plan to do to her. The way she felt wrapped around me at the trail has been seared into my mind.

Tight, wet, warm, and a damn perfect fit. Like we were made to meld together.

I can't miss out on the opportunity to feel that again...or let all those tedious hours I spent in here go to waste, so it's time to go get her.

Celeste

I would not have taken so many goddamn hits in that graveyard, if I had known I'd be trying to make my way out of a maze tonight. I've been lost since the second turn and it all looks the fucking same to me in the dark. *Probably would in the daytime too, let's be fucking for real.*

"Ugh!," I huff out in frustration before freezing in place. *Shit. What if he heard that?*

...Yeah what if he did? You want to be caught.

And I do...but I also want to win. What can I say? I've always been a little competitive and I like the idea of beating Damian at one of his games. Wipe that smug smile off his face...and then sit on it.

The only sounds I hear in the stillness though are the rustle of the cornstalks. Carefully, I start to make my way forward on the path again. *I really have no idea where I'm going. At this rate, even if I avoid him until sunrise, I might have to walk straight through the corn to get out before it opens to the public.* Suddenly, I look down at my blood-soaked clothes and a whole new realization hits me.

If we get caught in here, we are facing far more than trespassing charges. Shit.

The renewed panic has me picking up the pace and jogging along the path. *Left. Right. Right. Straight. Left...*I skid to a stop as I come up on a dead end. *Damn.* Turning around, I head back to the right and then stop. There are three paths off this stretch of maze. *Which one did I come from? I took a right into here...didn't I?*

I'm standing in the middle of the trail, questioning my entire existence at this point, when I hear it. Footsteps crunching over the dried out corn stalks that litter the ground. *Damian.* Instinctually, I squat down...behind nothing. *I'm too fucking high for this shit.* I start to tiptoe along the path, being careful to avoid debris as I listen. It sounds like he's somewhere on my right in the maze so I take the first turn on my left. *Just keep distance between you both until dawn...then you can yell for him to get you out of this fucking place before anyone else shows up.*

I creep down the path, breathing a little easier after I take yet another turn. It shouldn't be hard to do this as long as I listen carefully and keep heading in the opposite direction. *Easy. As long as I focus.*

A loud rustling, right next to me, makes me jump and let out a quick squeal. A small field mouse scurries over the ground in front of me, disappearing into the stalks on the other side. *Really, Celeste? A mouse made you yell? Get your shit together. No wonder the pot heads always die in horror movies.*

The sudden crashing of rapid footfalls sounds like thunder over the field. *Fuck! He heard me.* I take off, full-speed, deeper into the maze. I try to listen for him, but the stomps are too loud, echoing in the night. It's impossible to tell which way they're coming from. I'm taking random turns too quickly to keep up with which way I'm coming or going.

My pulse is pounding in my ears, adrenaline coursing through my veins, as I hit another dead end. *Damn it!* I spin on my heels, running for the first turn ahead of me. The corn debris is flying from under my feet as I skid around the turn and almost run head first into the dark, blood soaked, hulking figure before me.

Damian is standing in the path, still and waiting. *Like he was expecting me.* He's wearing the pumpkin mask again and the chill that runs through me at the mere sight makes my nipples harden. "...Ohhh, hi, Damian. You lost too?" I say as I start to slowly step back onto the path I came from.

His dark chuckle, corrupted by the voice changer, mixes with the rustling of the corn in a soundtrack to some twisted nightmare. Shaking his head slowly side to side, he says, "I'm not Damian in this mask. You are always my Sweet, Celeste. But I'm going to do things to you that no man with a conscience ever could, so this is the face of your demon, my Sweet. I want you to be able to look at me in the morning...without melting into a perfect slutty little puddle every time." I can hear the smug smile behind the mask.

But he's right. I'm a mess for him and his dark games...*and I wouldn't have it any other way.*

My voice trembles with excitement as I clear the corner of the turn and stand in the middle of the previous path, "Well you can't do anything, demon or not, if you can't catch me!" Taking off suddenly to the right, I'm high-kneeing it as fast as I can. The glow of the very whisper of sunrise is starting to warm the darkness. *Come on, Celeste, you've almost done it.*

But he's running after me, I can hear the thuds of his steps and they are close. *Too close.* I see a large opening ahead of me. *Is that the exit?* I pump harder, my chest bouncing and a sweat breaking out despite the cool air. He's right behind me but I can't risk a look back, even a second of hesitation could cost me the win.

Ten more feet. Fucking move! I close the distance faster than I ever have in my life.

Relief floods my body as soon as I pass through the opening, gasping and trying to catch my breath, only to be immediately replaced with dread. I'm still surrounded by corn, it's just a round clearing with multiple paths out. *Sh-*

He collides with me roughly, tackling me to the ground. The impact stuns me, but he doesn't slow in his attack, flipping me onto my back and crawling over me. His growl rumbles in the space between us, "Caught you, Witch. You're. All. Mine. Now."

Damian...*no, my Pumpkin Prince*...wrestles my hands in front of me and clasps both my wrists with one of his. His grip is powerful, dominating...and I already want to submit to him. But I can't. That's too *easy. Go to the grave as annoying as fucking possible...even when you enjoy it.*

I try to fight back, but I can't break his hold. Instead, I look up at him and say, "Hey, Pumpkin Face!"

He pauses for just a moment, but that's all I need. I spit onto the mask and watch it roll down the latex slowly. He hisses, but the twitch in his cock, that's pressed tight against me, makes it clear he likes my defiance.

Roughly, he pulls a silk rope from his pocket and begins to wind it around my wrists. "You," one loop, "shouldn't," another loop, "have," a third, "done that!" He jerks the tie tight, emphasising his point.

I simply smirk in response. "Why not? If I'm going to be punished, I might as well be rude and earn it."

He coils the rope around itself, binding me securely before pulling it over my head like a lead to pin my arms above me. Reaching behind himself, he produces the hunting knife and waves it in warning. "Stay still, my Sweet, or else this time the blade might end up inside you."

"You wouldn't" I gasp out in shock.

"Want to bet? I know how to stitch a wound very well, Witch." He runs the cold steel down my chest, making me tremble as he lets go of the rope. With the other hand, Damian jerks my t-shirt aggressively, pulling it up and over my chest and head, bunching it on my forearms.

Suddenly, he stabs the knife into the ground next to us, startling a jump out of me. Both his hands are on my waistband, making quick work of my button and zipper. My Pumpkin Prince tugs my jeans off me quickly. They peel away from my skin due to how soaked through they are with blood. Tossing them aside, he snatches the blade back up and cuts through my panties and bra, turning them into scraps and leaving me naked.

The cool air prickles my skin, bringing up goosebumps. He stands, stripping out of his own clothes as the sunrise begins to paint the sky behind him, showcasing his massive build and the stunning artwork that decorates him. Fully naked and hard, just for me. *He is fucking delicious.*

As he starts to kneel down to me again, I seize the opportunity to throw myself at him, knocking him backwards and climbing on top. I place all my weight onto my bound fists, that are curled up on his chest, pinning him.

"What's this, Witch?" he questions as his hands naturally find their way to my thighs, squeezing their flesh possessively.

"You may have won the chase, but I'm still going to take what I want...*like a Goddess should.*" I smirk at him, winking as I start to lower myself onto him.

"Well by all means, who am I to deny a deity?" He relaxes, putting his arms behind his head and laying back. Even through the mask, I can feel his eyes burning over my skin as he watches me.

I grind down against him, until his throbbing cock is lining up with my opening. As soon as his bulbous head presses against me, I groan and sit down farther, pushing it deep inside. My walls stretch over his thick member, massaging it, as we both moan out in unison. Our pants making a chorus together.

"You feel like heaven. *Fuck.*"

I pull up slowly, savoring the way I cling to him, before I slide back down, taking him deeper. My wrists being bound in front of me are forcing my breasts together, making them pillow out over my arms lewdly. With every steady gyration I make, he groans out and it is driving me wild. The sounds of his pleasure spur me on.

I place more pressure on my hands and start to bounce on his cock enthusiastically, hard enough to make my ass ripple against him with every impact. *Oh fuck, he feels so good inside me.* He is filling every inch of me. The pleasure has my eyes rolling back in my head as the delicious tingles start to shoot along all of my nerves. "Oh...yes!" I squeal out as my excitement builds. However, all the sensations are overpowering and my pace is beginning to stutter.

Immediately, his hands fly to my waist, gripping me hard, and lifting me up and down on his cock. He's helping me maintain my passionate rhythm without having to lose my pleasure to thought or concentration. I'm gasping in need as my orgasm builds.

"Fuck, Celeste. Don't stop." His voice is husky as he begins to pound back up into me. The need in him is swelling as well. "You fucking beautiful mess of a witch, don't you dare stop." His deliciously savage and frenzied thrusts are hurtling us both towards the edge.

I don't know *exactly* how loud I was when I came, but I know birds scattered into the morning light as I peaked. My body shook so hard on top of him that he had to hold me steady as the pleasure rolled over me in waves. Fed by his growls as he spilled inside me and my pussy spasmed around his cock, working it for every drop. *That was incredible.*

My mind is still foggy as Damian brushes the sweaty hair back from my face and frees my hands of rope and shirt. He rolls us gently onto our sides, so I can rest as he stands to dress himself. Damian collects the other scattered pieces of my bloody clothes, before bending back down to scoop me up into his arms. I look up at him, wrapping my own around his shoulders as he carries me through the maze.

Tenderly, I reach up and pull the mask from his head. I enjoy my perfect Pumpkin Prince - *greatly.* But I *love* this man and it's his face I want to see awash in the beautiful colors of the sunrise.

Damian glances down at me, that devastating smile on his face. "Let's go home, my Sweet."

Home with him...with my true self...sounds like my personal heaven as well.

Damian

Balancing a giant bowl of popcorn, multiple boxes of candies, a couple drinks, and a blanket is already difficult without Osiris weaving between my feet, but I manage to make it back to the theatre without creating a mess. Celeste is bent over, scouring the shelves for the perfect movie to start our Halloween slasher marathon with, flashing me that beautiful, full ass from underneath my favorite little witch costume. Looking just like she did the first time I saw her, with only the addition of the first quarter moon necklace I gifted her a few months back. Who said you had to leave the house to dress up?

She looks even more enrapturing in it this year, glowing from being in *her* house, with *her* movies, and in *her* element on *her* favorite day. I'm truly spellbound and I know how lucky I am to share this night with her. Especially to be able to let every part of me revel in the mischief with every side of her. The mask and knife are already hidden in the bathroom so I can surprise her later in the night, amid one of the bloodier scenes that really gets her going. But I have a feeling she's suspecting it since she made me promise not to do anything to ruin the costume.

She picks the original *Hellraiser*. *Oh yeah, she's planning to play games tonight, this one always works her up.* She pops in the DVD and comes to curl up in the same double recliner I'm in. She lays so she is propped up on the armrest, her hips on one seat, and her legs laid over my lap in the second, with her feet hanging off the other side. Osiris jumps up and snuggles into her chest. *Good spot, buddy.*

She looks like a living sculpture. Art of a young, alluring witch who has all the pleasures and joys of the world to offer someone. The kind of image that the church would've villainized and used to shame people into fear and submission. To deny them the happiness of this life, with the promise of rewards for their suffering in the next one. Because the beauty and force in women like her, the ones who own themselves completely - mind, flesh, pleasure, influence, darkness, and light - terrify those in power. Celeste has stepped into her place as a Goddess and she could topple empires if it suited her. Hers is the only name I will ever worship again.

I'm glowing from just being in her presence when my phone dings with a "Happy Halloween" message from Sam. He was pissed when I called him two weeks ago for that clean up. He hadn't done one in nearly fifteen years, but that man will have connections till the grave and there is no one else I would trust with it. Especially now, when I actually have something to lose by getting caught. In the last two weeks,

Issac's phone has traveled up the East Coast, pinging off multiple towers. His car, being driven by someone who looks a lot like him, has stopped in at a couple motels, where his ID and credit cards were used. Then a few nights ago, a homeless man turned his cellphone in saying that it had been left behind on the street next to an abandoned car on the bridge. He didn't see him jump, but there was a suicide note typed out on the phone explaining how he had destroyed his relationships with his parents and friends, and when his ex-girlfriend wouldn't take him back either, that there was no where left in the world that he belonged. They haven't recovered his body while dragging the river yet, but they'll give up in a few days. It's not uncommon to never retrieve a bridge jumper, especially those that do it into rivers near where they feed into the ocean. Of course, that's not where he really is, but I know Sam well enough to trust that's a body that'll never be found.

After I explained exactly who Issac was to Celeste and what he'd done to her, Sam seemed to be on board no problem. However, he did still make me listen to a lecture on how I cannot kill *all* her exs and he won't be helping me with another one. Even though we both know it's a lie. Sam and I have each other's backs to the end, no matter how much we might grumble about it along the way. But I wouldn't put him in that position again, unless absolutely necessary. Sam sacrificed alot to leave the life to begin with and then risked his fucking neck once more to get me out. But Issac had to go...he had to. *Retribution, as mother would say. It comes for all sinners.* Well fuck her and her God, I'm going to find refuge in my heaven for as long as I can before my sins catch up to me. I wrap one arm around Celeste's legs and rest the other on the armrest, ready to settle in for the movie and the coming night of chaos and sexy fun when my phone buzzes again.

I check it, expecting another message from Sam, but instead I'm greeted with an unknown number, "Happy Halloween to you and your witch. Play house while you can, cuz. I know that demon is gonna get restless sooner or later."

The End

Damian and Celeste will
return as main characters in
Cleansed by the Pyre
The Unrepentant : Book Three

More Tales
By
Olyvia Wyld
Coming Soon...

Goddess Made Flesh
The Unrepentant : Book Two

A Dark Sapphic Romance

Savannah Ward is a bold, loud, and unapologetic woman. She owns her sexuality and her body in a way that many women don't have the confidence to, none the less as a lesbian cam girl from a small Christian-Conservative town. But surviving in that world and overcoming those fears are what forged her into the force she is today. *Granted*, a force that has commitment issues, plays men for money and women for sex, and never plans to settle down,
but a force either way.
Savannah gets what she wants. Period.
So how dare the sexy, dark-haired, statuesque owner of Pantheon, her favorite queer club, steal her date?
Like she'd ever let her get away with that.

Aris Sagona has been watching the tiny little redhead work her way through half the women that frequent her club for years.
Never seriously invested, but always intrigued by her.
Savannah thinks what she wants is meaningless sex and fleeting distractions when Aris knows what she *needs* is discipline, submission, and the kinds of pleasures that only come from someone knowing your every secret and sinful desire.
But she's also aware that Savannah needs a taste of humility and to come to this realization on her own if this is ever going to work so Aris is about to make Savannah chase her...
Whether it drives the woman crazy in the process, isn't her problem.

Forbidden Fruit

A Sacreligious Dark Romance

Renae sold her own soul nearly sixty years ago just so she could damn
lying, manipulative, lechers herself and she's never regretted it.
She's one of the most successful Succubi walking the world today, so
after a mistake puts her contract at risk she's desperate to fix it.
However, now she's bound to her original human form, has limited
powers, and has been dropped off in the town she ran away from
when she was human.
But ever the go-getter, she sets her goals high.
"They want a soul that was devoted to another God as penance?
Fine, I'll bring them a priest"

Father Peter Levine spent practically his entire life preparing to
become a priest. God has always been there for him and his family, so
as far as he is concerned, the only way to repay the miracles laid upon
them is through a life of devotion and service.
He's settled happily into the small town of Laurelcrest,
ready to serve his Lord and this community as their priest,
when in walks a beautiful woman with a lost, wandering soul seeking
understanding and enlightenment.
But something unholy seems to reside behind that innocent face.
In 1st Corinthians 10:13 it is said "God is faithful; He will not suffer
you to be tempted beyond that which ye are able to bear."
So why now is God bringing a seductress who looks at the Father like
she might eat him alive into his flock?
He has never been so plagued by lustful thoughts and lecherous
desires before and it might just cost him his salvation.

The Daydreams of a Sexually Repressed Accountant

A Kinky 2000s RomCom Novella

Like most people, Hannah Brooks is laying in bed on Sunday night dreading having to go to work in the morning.
Like most people, she resolves to try a new way to entertain herself while there.
Unlike most people, she decides the best way to do that is to write down all her wild, kinky fantasies while on the clock.

Who knows? Maybe she'll come up with the next great smutty romance hit...or she'll end up in a meeting with HR.

Either way, she needs to keep this on the downlow.
Her boss, Elliot Harris, may be kind of cute, but he has absolutely no sense of humor.

Other people screw around on the clock all of the time.
Writing about screwing around, while on the clock, shouldn't be any harder...right?

Acknowledgements

Honestly, I don't know where to begin here. I am in awe of the people in my life and those who I have met throughout this journey. 'Lucky' doesn't begin to describe what I am to have been surrounded by such an incredible group of humans, who have believed in and supported me, as I took this dive.

First, thank you to my family. You have sacrificed time, energy, and finances so that I could do this. Even doing so enthusiastically, so I wouldn't feel like a burden. Y'all tended to every doubt and tear that came along during this process. Y'all made sure I ate and drank when I would get too lost in the work to remember on my own. Y'all even endured listening to every chapter twenty-five times out loud as I self-edited. I never would've reached this milestone without you. This is as much your victory as mine.

I also want to thank my close friend, Sorena, for all the precious time and energy she put into being my first editor, especially since this is not her genre. *She loves my twisted ass even if she would castrate my taste in men.* The commentary was incredible, your skills on point, and your friendship invaluable. *Also, I am incredibly sorry for my poor relationship with commas.*

Next, I want to thank my incredible PA Rachel and the effervescent coven of Wyld Witches she brought together. You are all bright, stunning mystics and so valuable to the success and spirit of *Spellbound*. I have been privileged to have met and worked with you all and I hope to do so again. Rachel was my sanctuary in the strange and foreign lands of social media, book marketing, and the book community. I can't explain to you how much my life changed as an author the day she reached out to me. Thank you, Rachel. Without you and the witches, I would still be lost in the digital woods screaming about this book into the void. You are all incredible.

Also, if you were a beta or ARC reader, thank Rachel because I had NO idea how to set any of that up.

Last, but certainly not least, I want to thank the other incredible contributors to *Spellbound*. My second editor Alysha Thornton, my cover artist Samantha Bishop, and my formatter Katiee Comer. Y'all are so pleasant and talented, it has been an absolute pleasure to work with you and I look forward to doing it again soon!

About The Author
Olyvia Wyld

Olyvia has done many things throughout her life, from creating escape rooms and acting in haunts to becoming a scientist and assisting in research, from working in a tattoo shop and as a cocktail waitress to performing in fetish shows and being an advocate for women's sexual and bodily autonomy. But the one thing that has stayed constant is a deep desire to connect and understand the world around her - the natural one, along with all the cultures and people who live in it. Now as she enters a fresh chapter of her own life, she is beginning another one of her dream adventures - becoming an author.

When she's not writing, you can find her exploring nature, spending time with her beautiful family, and seeing if she can convince Lillith to make Shadow Daddies a real thing.

Follow her for updates on upcoming novels and events on Instagram and Threads @olyviawyld

www.ingramcontent.com/pod-product-compliance
Lightning Source LLC
Chambersburg PA
CBHW020403110726
47899CB00006B/1846